Murder at the Blue Oyster Grill

by

Sandra Madden

Murder at the Blue Oyster Grill

COPYRIGHT © 2023 by Sandra Madden

Cover Art by *Lisa Dawn MacDonald*

The Wild Rose Press, Inc.
PO Box 708
Adams Basin, NY 14410-0708
Visit us at www.thewildrosepress.com

Publishing History
First Edition, 2023
Trade Paperback ISBN 978-1-5092-5185-8
Digital ISBN 978-1-5092-5186-5

Published in the United States of America

Honey Mayhew and her sister Cricket reached the crime scene in record time.

They ducked under the bright yellow tape in unison and made for the open door of the Blue Oyster Grill.

"Oh, come on now," Leo the deputy sheriff groaned, but he made no effort to stop them.

Eli! Eli Gibson. Honey's breath caught in her throat. The hot, oh-so-handsome sheriff stood in the center of the room. Her heart knocked against her chest in a series of jarring thumps. Nerves, she told herself. Any attraction she'd ever felt for the man had died long ago. Years and…many tears ago.

Suck it up. Face him. Get the story. The future depends on it.

Straightening her shoulders, she headed straight for the sheriff's rugged frame, hoping to project the look of a confident journalist. Not the internal quivering hot mess she felt.

With hands on his hips and feet planted apart, Blue Oyster Bay's sheriff towered over the chef's body. A frown of concentration etched his darkly tanned face as he studied the corpulent form of the deceased.

"Hey, Sheriff," Honey's greeting was barely audible and carefully casual as she stopped at Eli's side. Rather than make eye contact, she steeled herself and gazed down at the body. The town's favorite chef looked as if he were sleeping on the cracked tile floor. A chill ran through her. She'd never seen a dead body before.

Look away. Look away.

Praise

Dedication

To Alexandra,
My daughter. My best friend.

The Blue Oyster Banner

Dear Readers,

We invite you to subscribe to the Blue Oyster Bay Banner.

The Banner is a bi-weekly newspaper serving our community, the delightful panhandle town of Blue Oyster Bay, Florida. Family owned for fifty years, the Banner is published every Tuesday and Friday in the old school print tradition. The Blue Oyster Bay Banner proudly offers our residents news and information that most cannot get elsewhere and is available at a nominal cost by a caring staff that lives and works in Blue Oyster Bay.

In addition to home delivery, the Banner is available at the newspaper office, Rick's Ice Cream Shop, Astrid's Art Depot, Nicholson's Hardware store and Baytime Marine depot.

Purchase your copy now and read the story behind the latest headline:

MURDER AT THE BLUE OYSTER GRILL

Chapter 1

Sweet tea and grits! What was she doing here? How had she landed back in Blue Oyster Bay?

A warm rush of blurring tears gathered behind Honey Mayhew's eyes. Her silent and totally rhetorical question had brought her to the brink of a good cry. Something she mustn't do. Besides, she knew the answer. She'd failed, and that's why she was right back to where she'd started from. She'd failed. Failed. And failed again.

Seated at the computer on a non-ergonomic chair with one wheel missing, giving her a slightly lopsided view of the screen, Honey did not appear stressed—to the naked eye. And yet her heart slammed against her chest in a series of alarming palpations. She inhaled deeply, silently coaxing herself to calm down and get a grip.

It could be worse, after all. She could be incarcerated in a Third World Country.

Honey stared at the flashing cursor and blank blue screen of her computer—an ancient computer purchased during the time of cavemen and flying dragons. She released a sigh of frustration. She'd been sighing heavily at thirty-second intervals while blinking back tears. She didn't belong in Blue Oyster Bay. There were no blue oysters. In fact, since the oil spill there were very little oysters of any color or size. In addition, her job was a joke. And the blank screen refused to fill itself.

She glanced at the older, but amazingly attractive, woman across the room. "Momma."

"Mmmhmm." Laura Mayhew did not raise her eyes from the screen. She was all business all the time in the newspaper office. Despite being an admitted workaholic, she still managed at fifty-five years of age to resemble a young and adorable Southern belle. Honey admired her mother in so many ways but one.

"This is insanity, Momma. We need to take the Banner online. Modernize. The internet is where readers expect to find the news. We're struggling to keep a small-town print newspaper afloat while huge, respected papers are folding all across the country."

Her mother, owner, publisher, editor-in-chief of the *Blue Oyster Bay Banner*, looked up from her computer screen. Peering over her bifocals, her electric blues cut Honey with the look that had struck fear in her heart from the time she'd been old enough to walk. "Like the newspapers that laid you off, darlin'?"

Her mother's sweet tone denied the anger flashing in her eyes.

Suppressing another sigh, Honey nodded slowly. Sadly.

"Blessings in disguise," her mother uttered dismissively and returned to her editing.

Conversation concluded, Honey reviewed her blessings. The first so-called blessing came from the venerable Boston newspaper where she'd begun as an intern and worked her way up to her dream job as reporter for the arts pages.

Oh, how she'd loved that job!

Honey received her second blessing from a national

2

newsmagazine boasting a circulation in the millions. Well, there were those who called *The Weekly Spin* a tabloid, but there was no sense in arguing semantics now.

Just as counting her blessings was about to sink her further into a deep blue depression, the door burst open, and her younger sister blew in--almost literally.

"Chef Andy's dead!" Cricket shouted. She raced toward Laura's desk as if she was being chased by T-Rex. "He's been murdered!"

"Murdered?" Honey repeated. Her younger sister, the drama queen of the family, tended toward exaggeration in all things. "What? Did he run out of the lunch special?"

Cricket pointed wildly, finger stabbing the air in the general direction of the Blue Oyster Grill. Her long blond hair fell in a wild tangle, and her sun-bronzed body glistened with perspiration. "Every cop car in town is over there!"

Honey's sister qualified as a beauty, possessing a near-perfect figure, most always showcased in short-shorts and halter tops. The twenty-two-year-old could have been mistaken for a pro football cheerleader, compared to Honey's nerd-on-the-run look. Still a kid-at-heart, Cricket just couldn't decide what she wanted to be when she grew up.

"Every cop car? Do you mean all three patrol cars are there?" Honey asked. She couldn't help herself. Sometimes sarcasm seemed the only way to save her sanity. "One of the diners must have found a shell in their scrambled eggs."

Laura Mayhew's eyes narrowed to a death stare. "Honey, get over to the Grill now."

Courting disaster, Honey rolled her eyes. "Really?

3

A murder in this town?"

"Go. Check it out."

"Murder does not happen here."

"Honey!"

"Right." This investigation would be over before it started. Despite being away for six years, Honey knew Blue Oyster Bay and its residents well. She'd be back in the office in less time than it took to write a weather report. Sunny and hot as blue blazes.

"Cricket, you go too—and take the camera," Laura ordered.

Cricket's amber eyes went wide. "You want me to take pictures of a dead body?"

"No."

"But—"

Honey snatched her tablet from the desk, slammed her wide-brimmed, beat-up, old floppy straw hat on her head and gave her younger sister a gentle shove. "We'll find something for you to aim your camera at. Let's go."

Her given name had always embarrassed Honey, but her sister's Cricket moniker was so much worse. She wondered what her mother might have been thinking when she named her children. Honey also figured her sister had the larger cross to bear.

The Blue Oyster Grill sat on the corner of Main Street only a block and a half away.

As soon as the newspaper office was out of sight, Honey slowed down.

Cricket shot her a questioning look. "We should hurry. Why are you slowing?"

"It's way too hot to hurry. You know about heatstroke, right?"

"Old Mrs. Killean had one last year." Cricket raised

her camera and snapped. "Almost croaked."

"It could happen to us too. At any minute. And *puleeze,* put that camera down. Don't be taking pictures of me."

"I want proof. I still can't believe you're back home."

"That makes two of us."

Honey's career—her life—seemed as washed up as the dank seaweed strewn along the beaches of Blue Oyster Bay. The small town where she'd been raised, and fled from as soon as possible, lay just south of Alabama and a stone's throw north of the Gulf of Mexico. Her hometown was southern poor and scenic rich, with vibrant blue skies and sparkling white sand beaches leading to the aquamarine bay.

Taking in the downtown scenery as they strolled, Honey admitted feeling some pride in Oyster Bay; she just didn't want to be trapped in the one-traffic-light town. Seriously, one light. Designated an historic area, Blue Oyster Bay was also known as the best kept secret on the Forgotten Coast—for good reason.

Seeped in southern plantation history, the small town had been settled on the far western slice of the Florida Panhandle at the mouth of the Apalachicola River. Back in the day, the fishing industry as well as cotton export contributed to the town becoming a major Gulf port. Hundreds of bales of cotton were shipped down the river on steamboats and stored in the brick warehouses that lined the Apalachicola River. Ultimately the bales were loaded on vessels bound for their final destinations of New York and Boston.

These days, not a sprig of cotton could be seen in the "Bay," as the locals referred to their slice of paradise.

Most of the residents tonged for oysters to earn what amounted to an extremely meager living. But not Honey. She toiled at above minimum wage for her mother— apparently the only person in North America who would hire her.

Dreading the death scene for what she assumed to be a non-story, Honey took a deep breath of the salty air, mostly to steady the rocks roiling around deep within her belly. Dragging her heels wasn't enough to avoid the inevitable, especially with Cricket all eager to arrive at the Grill.

"Momma's gonna kill us if we don't get this story. Come on, let's get a move on," Cricket urged, barely suppressing her excitement. "At this rate the body will be gone by the time we get there."

"The body? Have you not a shred of respect for the man?"

She hung her head. "Sorry. Chef Andy."

"And why risk sunstroke because the poor man suffered a heart attack?"

"We won't know why he died until we get there."

"I can assure you, Little Sister, he was not murdered."

Cricket came to an abrupt halt. "Oh."

"What, oh?"

"Eli will be there. He's the reason you're not in a hurry to get to the Grill."

"Is that what you think?"

Giving Honey her best smirky sister smile, Cricket replied. "Yes, that's what I think."

"Why should I care if Eli's at the Grill?" Honey asked, shaking her head, ignoring her trembling hands. *But she did.* She did care. A lot.

Cricket snorted.

Honey ignored her.

Was it too late to turn back? Yes. Way too late. She could not avoid Eli now after she'd spent the last six weeks carefully avoiding the man. And what if poor Andy's death turned out to be more of a story than she thought? A story that might prove to be her ticket out of Blue Oyster Bay?

In less than five—sister silent—minutes they reached the Grille on the corner of Main and Third Street, the site of the town's only intersection.

Honey nodded and gave a bright smile to the deputy sheriff, Leo Jones. Leo returned the nod as he wrapped crime scene tape around the restaurant and adjoining sidewalk. A few dozen tourists and townspeople milled about, attempting to see what was happening inside the Grill that required taping the restaurant off.

Honey and Cricket ducked under the crime scene tape in unison and made for the open door of the Grill.

"Oh, come on now," Leo groaned, but he made no effort to stop them other than hunching his shoulders forward in a disappointed slump.

Eli! Eli Gibson. Honey's breath caught in her throat. The hot, oh-so-handsome sheriff stood in the center of the room, tall and solid as Florida Pine. Her heart knocked against her chest in a series of jarring thumps. Nerves, she told herself. Just nerves. Any attraction she'd ever felt for the man had died long ago.

However. Frozen in place, she couldn't move. Her throat had gone dry. Her feet felt as if they were bolted to the floor. She really shouldn't stare but she couldn't seem to tear her gaze away. It had been so long since she had seen him. So many years and…tears ago.

Cricket nudged her in the back. Honey could stall no longer. *Got to suck it up. Got to face him. Got to get the story. Her future might depend on it.*

Straightening her shoulders, she headed straight for the sheriff's rugged frame, hoping to project the look of a competent, confident journalist, rather than the internal quivering mess she felt. Annoyingly, Cricket clipped along at her heels.

With hands on his hips and feet planted apart, the Bay's sheriff towered over the dead chef's body. A frown of concentration etched his darkly tanned face as he studied the corpulent form of the deceased.

"Hey, Sheriff," Honey's greeting was barely audible and carefully casual as she stopped at Eli's side. Rather than make eye contact, she steeled herself and gazed down at the body. The town's favorite chef looked as if he were sleeping on the cracked tile floor. A chill ran through her. She'd never seen a dead body before.

Look away. Look away.

"Is…is Andy really dead?" she asked quietly, as if afraid she might wake the sleeping chef.

"Appears so," Eli answered without looking at her.

Honey's stomach rolled over in a sickening series of tumbles as she stared at the corpse. She'd never covered a murder or any story involving a death before. But she couldn't look away, could not summon the nerve to look at Eli either. She swallowed hard, forcing down the bile, and turning her attention to Cricket.

Her sister's hands shook as she raised the camera, preparing to aim and shoot.

Honey closed her eyes. This wasn't right. None of it. The tension in the air swelled like a balloon ever closer to the cringing pop that would send balloon shards sailing in all directions. Andy, one of the Bay's outstanding citizens, lay on the floor unmoving. The taciturn sheriff continued to study the body while very obviously, totally, and unnecessarily ignoring her. Awkward.

A man she had once known so well had become a stranger. A stranger wearing a short-sleeved light brown khaki sheriff's uniform. Very different from the uniforms she'd seen him wear in the past. A gold star badge gleamed on his chest. That was different too, yet the familiar scent of Eli filled her senses with man, sea, and forest. Woodsy. The disturbing combination electrified the space between them, triggering memories of the misunderstandings, loneliness, and pain.

When had his shoulders broadened? When had the small lines of his face etched deeper and his skin darkened to sun-leathered ruggedness?

The *click-click-click* of Cricket's digital camera split the tense silence between Honey and Eli.

"Stop," Eli barked.

A meek, "Sorry," followed from Cricket.

With a whoosh of relief, Honey snapped out of her emotional foray. Despite fate or whatever had brought both her and Eli back to Blue Oyster Bay, back to the Blue Oyster Grill today, they each had a job to do. She could not allow the fact she hadn't seen or spoken to him in six years to interfere with the story of the poor dead chef. Whatever the story might be.

After sending up a prayer for Andy, literally the big man around town, she went to work. Just after a month since her return to her hometown, Honey might at last have stumbled on a story. If it really was a story, perhaps one of the wire services would pick it up. A worldwide news network maintained a small office in Tallahassee, only an hour's drive away. Hope slowly blossomed in her heart, and with hope came courage.

She risked weak knees and possible heart failure as she glanced up at Eli. His familiar mouth, his stormy sea eyes, and his once-broken nose had all been imprinted on her heart and mind years ago. Unchanged, his features merged into a heart-stopping whole.

Clearing her sandpaper throat, she asked, "How did Andy die? Did he have a heart attack?"

"Don't know yet." The sheriff's gaze remained fixed on the body.

Chef Andy was a big man. Or had been. Honey guessed he weighed at least three hundred pounds. Clearly, he'd taste tested every dish he created for years. He was dressed in the professional chef's uniform of black and white check trousers. The colors of the special of the day streaked his white jacket.

Honey was becoming impatient with Eli's awkward silences and abrupt replies. She'd come for a story; she needed a story. "Can food poisoning be fatal?" Honey suspected the obese chef had not always served the freshest ingredients, his kitchen not the cleanest. She'd eaten at the Blue Oyster Grill a time or two and done a brief investigation. She'd snooped while Andy was out.

"I'm thinking he had a heart attack," Cricket put in.

Eli shrugged. "Could be his heart gave out."

"But you don't suspect foul play?" Honey asked.

Eli shifted his gaze from Andy's body to Honey, blatantly taking in her hat, tee-shirt, faded shorts and flip-flops. He stopped at her chipped scarlet polished toes. "I don't speculate."

Do not talk to my toes! She protested silently,

painfully aware she did not present a big market city professional appearance. Her small-town appearance wasn't that fetching either. Pressing on, she asked, "But who would want to kill Chef Andy?"

"Who said anything about Andy being killed?" he snapped.

"So he hasn't been murdered?"

"Murdered? That's how rumors start." Eli let out an exasperated sigh and ran a hand through his longish chestnut hair. "We won't know the cause until we have an autopsy."

"So, I'll just say in my story that the sheriff has no idea of the cause of death. He's waiting for the medical examiner's report."

"That would be accurate."

"Who found him?"

"His wife. Thea." He shot Honey a dark, narrowed glance. "Are you finished with the questions?"

"No."

"I'm finished answering." Eli turned away.

Undaunted, Honey followed. "How long ago did she find him?"

Once again he came to an abrupt halt, turned back to her. "Thirty minutes or so."

"Poor Andy, this is just so…so tragic," Cricket put in. "Whatever, however it happened."

Honey agreed. "I am sorry. For Andy and for Thea."

"Do you know of anyone who would want to kill him?" Eli asked, making eye contact with Honey for the first time.

His question took her by surprise. "No! Goodness no. I hardly knew the man." Heat pooled in the back of her neck.

Eli cocked his head. "Heard you had an altercation with Andy recently."

Where had he heard that? Her cheeks grew warm. "No."

"Is that your final answer?"

"Yes." She slammed the cover of her tablet closed. "No. But calling a small squabble an altercation would be going a bit too far. It was a minor incident. Nothing important."

"Honey threatened to publish a restaurant report in the paper," Cricket told the sheriff with a bit more enthusiasm than Honey felt called for. "She's our investigative reporter and she threatened to let the whole town know there were live roaches crawling around in the kitchen. Cockroaches," Cricket clarified unnecessarily.

"As a public service. I wasn't being hateful." But if Honey were to be honest, she desperately had been attempting to drum up a story.

"A story like that in the paper would chase the Grill customers away," her sister observed in a righteous tone.

"Cricket! Can't you take a picture of something?"

Eli's forehead folded into a deep frown. "You were gonna do that? A roach report?"

She lowered her eyes. Her cheeks burned.

"Oh, man," he groaned.

"Live roaches are not healthy. Anywhere. Especially in a restaurant kitchen. I believe one of my duties as a journalist should be to warn the people of Blue Oyster Bay and…and our tourists of unhealthy conditions. One of the essential obligations of a journalist is to protect and inform the public."

"Man, oh, man." Eli shook his head. "How did Andy

react to your pending good deed?"

"He told me if I published the story, he'd kill me."

The sheriff's eyebrows shot up. "So maybe you just up and killed him first?"

Honey gasped. "No! How could you say such a thing?" she demanded, taken off-guard. "You can't be serious. You know I could never hurt anyone."

His jaw hardened as he turned his back on her and bit out the word, "Right."

But, oh! Wait! She had hurt him. Eli.

She closed her eyes. Took a deep breath.

"How is Thea taking it?" Cricket asked, stepping between Honey and Eli.

Honey drew a heart-calming breath, grateful for her sister's question. While Eli answered she took a moment to regroup and reclaim her investigative demeanor. She also wanted to know how Thea was handling the unexpected death of her husband. Thea, the chef's wife of twenty years worked alongside him in the restaurant.

"As you might expect, she's hysterical," Eli allowed, his tone soft and tinged with sympathy. He gestured with a nod of his head. "Carol took her over to Doc Fulton's to get a sedative."

Honey nodded. Carol Kahn worked at the Grill as the hostess and main server.

"Thea and Carol were back in the kitchen and heard Andy fall," Eli added.

"I was passing by on my way to the paper when I heard a thud and a few seconds later, Thea screamed," Cricket explained.

Incredulous, Honey turned to her sister, "You got that Chef Andy had been murdered just from passing by and hearing a thud and a scream?"

"Um hum." Cricket raised the camera, aiming at Eli.

Frustrated and feeling like this might be the worst interview of her entire journalistic career, an interview that would lead nowhere, Honey turned her attention to the man who least cared for her success, or failure. "Eli, were there any customers in the Grill when Andy…when he…he passed?"

"No. Too early. Hadn't opened for lunch yet."

Click.

"Cricket, put that camera away for Pete's sake," Eli barked.

"Sorry."

But the sheriff apparently had had enough of *Bay Banner*'s intrepid reporters. "You shouldn't be here," he said fixing a hard glare on Cricket. "Either of you." His head jerked in Honey's direction. "Get out and let me work."

Cricket scooted out the door, but Honey maintained her ground. "I hope you're not going to let, ah, personal feelings interfere with this…this investigation."

"This is not yet an investigation," he said turning away from her. "And I don't have any personal feelings."

Stung. An unexpected stab of pain cursed through her. His curt indifference made a direct hit on Honey's heart. But what could she expect? Straightening, she held her body rigid, her voice steady. "People deserve to know what happened to Andy. He was well-liked and a fixture in the community. I know you'll honor the public's right for any information."

"When I know something, the residents of Blue Oyster Bay, who I have vowed to serve and protect— now apparently, including you—will know."

He resented protecting her? Another arrow straight

to Honey's heart. Apparently, he was unable to let bygones be bygones and just be friends. She'd hoped to be friends. No, more than that, not lovers or best buds, friends.

She raised her chin. Although she might not feel it, she could show indifference as well. "Good. Then you'll call me."

"If you don't leave now, Ms. Mayhew, I'll arrest you."

"For doing my job? I'll be following this story until it's not a story, so I suggest you get used to seeing me." With a huff, she marched out. *Ms. Mayhew my eye!*

****

Eli watched Honey leave. When he'd heard that she'd returned to the Bay, his first thought was to turn in his badge and get out of town. Because.

Because he knew he couldn't control the feelings he'd buried deep inside of him. Because he'd known instinctively the second Honey hurried into the Grill. He'd always known when she was near. Eli never had to have eyes on her to know. It was a feeling. The girly, fresh-scrubbed lemon citrus scent of Honey had lingered in his memory since before he'd fallen in love with her. The spark in her light silver-blue eyes, the curve of her lips when she smiled, even the beguiling bounce of her sun-streaked curls had lived deep in his heart since the first time they'd held hands. He remembered how she used to cry both in sad movies and those with sappy happy endings, how she gave that funny smothered little snort when unable to contain her laughter. Eli remembered her well. He shook his head. Shaking her out of his thoughts. Nothing had changed. She'd always been headstrong, always been right...no matter the evidence to the contrary.

When Honey had marched into the Grill as if she'd owned it, his heart had dropped to his stomach. The palms of his hands grew wet with sweat. He'd known they'd run into each other sooner or later. Either theywould bump into each other on the street, or on the beach, or maybe in a quiet aisle of the grocery store. It was inevitable. Through the years, Eli had often wondered how he'd react to seeing her again. Now he knew. Sweaty palms.

Surreptitiously wiping his palms on his pants, he shook his head at the crazy timing. Just when he'd finally reached the point where he hardly thought of Honey Mayhew anymore–she was back. And she'd be trouble.

The only person he should be thinking about was the dead man on the floor, Andy Mueller. Andy wasn't Eli's best buddy, but he knew enough about culinarytrained chef. The man's big body contained what most folks considered a larger-than-life personality. He'd been a friend to Blue Oyster Bay, a friend to every customer.

Yeah, most likely a heart attack killed Andy this morning. Took his life too soon. There was no story for *Bay Banner's* intrepid, investigative reporter.

"Eli!" Leo called just as Eli's thoughts had begun to drift back to Honey. "Miz Carol called. She'd like a ride back from Doctor Owen for her and Miz Thea."

"Right." He had a job to do and an obligation to the law and the town's folks. "You stay here and keep a watch on things, Leo. I'll go to the doc's and pick up the ladies." He could use the time to ask a few more questions.

Thea and Andy lived in the apartment above the Grill. In order to protect Thea's privacy, Eli meant to pick up the women and usher them in the back door, assuming Carol would stay with Thea for a while. He refused to allow Honey Mayhew to mess up his mind.

Before leaving, Eli bowed his head in respect for Andy. He was gonna miss the man who took such pride in creating the best hush puppies on the Panhandle.

Andy would call in his big, deep, booming voice each time Eli walked through the door. "Hey there, Sheriff! What'll you have? It's on the house today."

Each time, Eli would reply, "Thanks Andy, but you know I can't accept favors. You serve the best oysters, and that's good enough for me." Eli always ordered the hush puppies on the side.

Actually, Andy didn't serve the best oysters or hush puppies, but the food was cheap and served fast. The Blue Oyster Grill was Eli's go-to for a quick bite to eat. Andy would come and sit with him until Eli's order arrived. The Grill's proud owner always told him a new, slightly off-color joke and laugh whether Eli found the humor or not. During baseball season they would talk baseball; in football season, they would argue football. Man stuff.

Eli was going to miss the big chef, as he believed most of the folks in town would. There'd be an autopsy as always in these cases, but he fully expected the medical examiner's report to say Andy died of a heart attack. Murder was unheard of in Blue Oyster Bay. It just wasn't done.

Although with Honey back in town, Eli supposed anything could happen.

Chapter 2

"Is Andy really gone?" Laura Mayhew asked as her daughter, Honey rushed through the door and straight to her computer. "Was it natural causes?"

Honey nodded. "Most likely. I doubt if there's a mystery about to unravel. No one in Blue Oyster Bay passes from anything but natural causes." *Or boredom.-*
.

"Stay on top of the story just in case."

"I will, Momma." Why not? Even though it was a nonstory she had little else to do. Perhaps following through with the story, in time she might convince Eli they could become friends again. Or would, if they found themselves together enough.

Laura tsked in her motherly manner, "Bless his heart…"

Eli?

"Andy was overweight," she added, "but that's a hazard when one works in the food industry, I suppose."

"Momma, do you want to see my pictures?" Cricket asked.

"Of course. You may turn out to be our number one photographer."

Honey groaned quietly.

Cricket flopped down in her chair, with all four wheels, did the digital download, and five minutes later made for the door. "My work here is done. See y'all!"

Her sister had obviously not been saddened for long by the chef's demise, although a cloud of depression had fallen over Honey. She had filed a nebulous story accompanied by the most flattering photo of Chef Andy she could find in the files and felt it wasn't enough.

Hours later, with no more news from the crime scene and running out of busy work, Honey prepared to leave the office. But not before checking with her mother. "Has Miss Bess come back from lunch yet?" Her grandmother, aka Miss Bess, wrote the obituary section. The eldest Mayhew preferred the grandma portion of her title be left unsaid.

"No." Laura frowned and shot Honey a rueful smile. "We'll just move obits to the next edition and include Andy's when we have the viewing and funeral information."

Lunch for Miss Bess was often an all-day event. Honey nodded. "Okay then. I'll call it a day."

"Would you like to come over for dinner tonight?"

"I'd love to, but I have so much work on the house to do." Honey put on her darn it face. "And a dog to walk." Which was a slight exaggeration. Fred was a hefty old bulldog who lumbered along when and if he chose to rise up and stand on all four legs.

When Honey had been forced to return to the Bay, she'd opted out of the family living arrangement in favor of being independent as she had been for several years. It was one thing to return home dragging her tail behind her and another to return to the bedroom ridden with high school posters, loser medals, traumas, angst…and memories of Eli.

She left by the back door. "See you tomorrow! Love you, Momma…"

After swapping her straw hat for a helmet, Honey climbed on her faded red '92 moped and barreled onto Highway 98 for the ten-minute ride to her rental home. Barreling along on her scooter meant reaching a speed of up to fifty miles per hour along the two-lane highway. The picture book scenery made up for her rough ride. On either side of the road high pines, palms and oaks formed a gnarly jungle. With each breath she tasted tangy salt, and the pungent scent of new forest growth, and old decay. It was not altogether unpleasant.

Honey's two-bedroom cedar shingled house stood on pilings overlooking the bay and sat just off the highway behind a thick growth of North Florida scrub. Except for the red tin roof, which gleamed under the sun and gave its presence away, the scrub concealed the beach house from the highway. Honey's grandmother had made the affordable rental arrangements. Once a realtor, Miss Bess knew everyone in town—and knew their business as well.

Once at home, Honey lived in isolation, a world away from prying eyes, alone with her shame. Not only hadn't she set the world on fire. She'd had not even managed to light a match.

She hated to turn down a dinner invitation. With the exception of Chef Andy, her momma and grandma were the best cooks in the county. Sadly, Honey had not inherited their cooking skills. But having dinner—or any other meal with her mother, grandmother, and sister—meant listening to their well-meaning warnings: At twenty-eight years old she was not getting any younger. Beauty was fleeting and her eggs would dry up tomorrow. If they hadn't already.

Blue Oyster Bay was a fine place to raise a family

with its sun, sand, and supportive relatives. The men who grew up in town and stayed were basically good men. Most might not be as educated or as smart as some of the men Honey had met in the city, but they were honest and hardworking men, important attributes in a husband.

Neither the conversation nor the warnings ever changed. Honey knew them by heart. Her attempts to sway her momma and Miss Bess into believing she found her life as a single woman fulfilling had not been successful. Especially now that she had a dog for a companion, but to this point in time her four-legged friend had proven more faithful than any man she'd known.

The aged American Bulldog who mainly snored and drooled had come with the fixer-upper house. She paid a minimal rent in return for her promise to repair and restore the house. Since the dog evidently had no name, she called him Fred. Just because she could.

Like many of his breed, the bulldog sported the jowls of the former British Prime Minister, Winston Churchill. Fred also possessed the body of a barrel and stubby legs, which he used as little as possible. Mostly he hung out in the shade of the veranda overlooking the Gulf and drooled.

Relieved to be home Honey hurried up the steep stairs to the veranda. "Hey, Fred!"

The dog opened his eyes but didn't move. "It's dinner time."

One of the few words he understood was "dinner." He hauled himself up on his stubby legs and waddled into the house after her. Although there was some light left in the dusky sky, she flipped on the light switch and surveyed the great room.

Not truly great in the truest sense of the word but it was a comfortably sized room consisting of a living, dining and kitchen unified by a distressed pine wood floor.

"It doesn't look like anyone lives here," she mumbled aloud to Fred.

Old dusty sheets covered the furniture which had come with the house. The only exception to the covers was one overstuffed recliner placed directly in front of the television set where she ate and watched news programs. Honey prided herself as a news junkie, a journalist who would be ready when called. If ever.

"I'm supposed to be fixing this house up, Fred. But it's hard to get motivated when you know it's only a temporary home."

Recently, Honey had purchased a soft, sea-glass green color paint and planned to paint the room herself. Any day now. As soon as she borrowed a ladder. And after she opened the moving boxes scattered throughout the room. Except with any kind of luck she would never have to open them at all. She'd be back in business and living in an invigorating city like Chicago or New York with like-minded professionals.

Away from Eli. And the flood of memories just seeing him had brought on. After all these years, she'd expected to be immune. Hadn't happened.

Fred sat on her left foot. He felt like a forty-pound lead weight. "Okay, I get it. You're hungry." She pulled her foot out from under him and moved into the kitchen to pour his dinner.

Honey's bedroom was one of two on the first floor separated by a bathroom. During her first week in the house, she'd painted the room a cool aquamarine shade that blended right into the Gulf waters just beyond the wall of glass windows. In time, she meant to refinish the wide plank wood floors. But that promised to be a huge job and she might not be living here all that long.

The second floor featured a loft. She seldom went up to the loft where more unopened boxes waited. No telling what she might find there.

As much as Honey's momma and Grandma Bess wanted her to stay in Blue Oyster Bay; is as much she longed to leave. More so after her disappointing encounter with Eli. Every night and on weekends at home she'd been writing feature pieces and a small-town blog in hopes of an internet company picking her up, hiring her to write content in some fabulous city, maybe Los Angeles.

After watching the news while downing a container of yogurt that might or might not have been past its expiration date by thirty days, Honey grabbed her laptop. Fred lay at her feet snoring, an oddly comforting sound. The curser blinked on the blank screen. Her eyes were growing heavy when she heard a thump. She started. A thump overhead. Wide awake now, Honey's throat went dry. Another thump.

Fred raised his head.

It wasn't her imagination. The bulldog had heard something too. And she suspected Fred was hard of hearing. Her heart began its own thump-thump rhythm.

Fred sniffed and looked slowly around the room. Drooling, he pushed himself up from the floor.

All was silent for the next minute. Honey held her breath. And then…thump.

She jumped. She and Fred were not alone.

And there might be a killer on the loose in town.

Her breath came in shallow gasps as she dashed on tiptoe to the counter where she picked up her cell phone and pushed the three buttons. 9-1-1...

"Sheriff's office."

She hadn't expected Eli to answer. Her heart fluttered to a stop. Her hands trembled, as did her voice.

"Eli," she whispered. "Send help quickly. Someone's in my attic."

She hung up. Heart racing, afraid to move, she listened. And heard nothing. Saw nothing. The night was coal black; no city streetlights illuminated the beach. No moonlight danced on shimmering Gulf waters. Seeking to calm her racing heart, she breathed deeply and armed herself with the only item close by that might possibly protect her—a three-pound doorstop in the shape of a squirrel and, of course, Fred.

Talking to him helped. "Come on, Fred. Get up, let's shed some light on the subject." Honey hurriedly turned on every lamp inside and outside of the beach house. The overweight watchdog ignored her whispered entreaties to hurry. He ambled behind her with an attitude of extreme nonchalance. To her major relief, no one jumped out at her. But her pulse pounded as if it would happen any minute. And she would be dead.

While she waited for help, Honey hid in the tiny bathroom with the breaching whales wallpaper. The wait became excruciating. Her imagination ran wild. Escape convicts hiding in the attic were preparing to drop through the access and pistol whip her while they pillaged the remains of her pantry and fridge. A serial killer had been camping quietly in the attic for weeks but was now in full desperate kill mode, bloodlust after murdering Chef Andy. Despite what he'd said on the phone Eli refused to come to her rescue. Why else would it be taking so long? Hunkered down in the bathtub shivering in fear, she was doomed.

Honey alternated between hyperventilating and not breathing at all. She'd always thought of herself as a brave new woman surviving heartbreak and freaking bad luck. She had survived single living in metropolitan cities and wrote—for a short time—with a byline for a national newspaper. How had she ended like this, cowering in a corner of a Blue Oyster Bay beach house? Because when she'd lost her job, she had done the only thing she could and returned home where she accepted the only job possible. The one offered by her mother. Honey became the investigative reporter for the family-owned newspaper, which had never needed one before, *the Blue Oyster Bay Banner*. The fact there hadn't been anything to investigate in town for thirty years or more did not seem to disturb her mother who'd hired her, no questions asked. No resume required.

Twenty exceptionally long minutes later by her count, her cell rang simultaneously with a pounding at the door. The cell registered the sheriff's phone number. Rescue at last! Creeping from her hiding place toward the beachfront door, she answered the cell. "H…h…hello?"

Fred followed closely, too closely, stepping on her bare heels. His toenails needed clipping.

"The door's locked. Let me in."

Eli's voice in stereo. In her ear. On the porch.

She hadn't expected *him*. She thought Eli would send Leo. Anyone in the police department other than the sheriff would have been welcomed. Honey hated the thought of Eli witnessing her as she was—a vulnerable, quivering hot mess.

She squared her shoulders.

Fred growled, a low ominous sound followed by a sharp bark. One bark led to another.

"Fred, hush!" After shooting the dog a death stare which surprisingly quieted him, Honey raised her chin and opened the door.

Frowning deeply, the sheriff stood framed under the yellow porch bug light. Wariness glinted in his eyes. A glint she'd earned, most likely. In the old days he might rightly have assumed she was up to something, like seduction or a loving prank. But that was then, and this was now.

Eli wasn't in uniform. Instead of his official khaki apparel he wore blue jeans, moccasins, and a plaid flannel shirt over a black tee-shirt that he'd apparently outgrown. The tee-shirt stretched tightly against his chest in a way she found slightly disturbing, and that she shouldn't be thinking about it at a time like this. The lean and wiry young man had become a muscular figure with wide, solid shoulders which could carry any weight, any worry. Shoulders a woman could lean upon. She was safe.

He wore his gun belt and carried a flashlight the size of bazooka. She smiled. She'd never felt afraid when Eli had been near. He'd not changed so very much. Most women wouldn't consider him handsome in the traditionally accepted way of chiseled features, cleft chin, and shadowed beard. But Eli's rough shorn looks emanated both sex appeal and strength, strength of body and character. Attributes that still attracted Honey. However, the square set of his jaw and the tight set of his lips suggested he might be extremely irritated at the moment.

"Thanks for coming. Eli, I'm sorry to drag you out at night."

"Yeah. Let's get this done." He brushed by her, his gaze sweeping the great room. "Where's the access to your attic?"

"I…I'm not sure."

"Fred couldn't find it for you?"

"Fred?" Oh. Eli had heard her yell at the dog, now drooling beside her. "No, he couldn't help," she explained. "Fred is my dog."

Eli looked down, eyed the dog for a brief moment, and scowled. "You named a dog Fred?"

"He's okay with it." She shot Fred a sweet smile, unlike any she'd given Eli to this point. "The access might be in the closet of the master bedroom. Or from the loft."

"I'll check the closet first." He motioned with a curt jerk of his head. "After you."

The set of his jaw tightened as they stood in her bedroom together. Awkward. Every nerve in her body tingled. Her cheeks burned. This scenario was disturbing in every way possible.

Hurriedly, she opened the small closet door. "Is that the access door up there?"

He moved to her side and looked up. She breathed deeply of his sea and woodsy scent.

The taciturn sheriff nodded. "Looks like that's it."

"Eli, I didn't mean to interrupt your night off. I expected Leo or another officer would answer the call."

"Really? We have a very small police department, in case you'd forgotten. I am where the buck stops."

"Of course," she nodded. Seeking to un-ruffle his

ruffled feathers Honey added, "I hope I didn't interrupt anything…important."

He grunted in response.

There weren't a lot of clothes in the closet. Honey had only unpacked one suitcase, hoping every day she would be hired from one of the thousands of *curriculum vitae* she'd mailed and emailed. Eli helped her pile the contents of the closet on the bed.

"Are you packing or unpacking?" he asked.

"Unpacking."

"Huh. Hard to tell."

Honey's throat went dry. "I've been busy. I'll get to it soon."

He stood in the now empty closet.

She held her breath.

"I don't hear anything," he said.

Honey held out her still shaking hands. "There were several loud thumps."

"Thumps," he repeated, swiping a hand through his slightly disheveled hair.

"Like someone was bumping around in the dark. Someone is up there," she insisted.

"Ssssh…I'm listening."

"Right." She held her breath and listened too.

Nothing.

"You're certain you heard something? Thumps?"

He didn't believe her. "Positive."

"Guess I better take a look," he said, pulling down the flimsy stairs. Aiming his flashlight up ahead of him, he climbed the stairs.

"Be careful."

Honey stood by the ladder listening. After holding her breath for a long moment, she heard a hiss. Startled, she squeaked. "What is it?"

Eli's muffled reply definitely wasn't directed to her. "Easy, there, easy."

"Eli, who…or what are you talking to?"

He backed down the stairs. "You've got a raccoon family in the attic."

"Are you just going to leave them there?"

"They won't give you a problem for now." Once his feet hit the floor he turned to her. "Alvin Gray is our critter catcher now. Give him a call in the morning and he'll come out and cage them for you."

She watched with grudging admiration as the sheriff she'd once adored pushed the folding stairs back into place with one hand. "Isn't this the old Carter place?"

"Yes. In return for a rock-bottom rental price, I'm fixing it up."

He gave the bedroom a cursory perusal. "Have you started the fixing yet?"

"I painted this room and I'll do the rest—soon."

"That'd be good. Hope you do. This beach house is a prime piece of property." With another curt nod, Eli strode out of Honey's bedroom and headed for the door.

She followed. "Thank you for coming. I appreciate it."

"It's my job."

"Can…can I get you anything? Before you go? Water, beer…"

"No." He'd reached the door. "No thanks."

She couldn't let him get away just yet. "Have you had any word on Andy from the ME?"

Eli's hand stilled on the doorknob. "No, the wheels of life, death, and justice spin slowly around here."

"You'll let me know?"

He turned the knob. She stood so close that with every breath she inhaled the pine woods, salt air scent of him. And she liked it. She liked the familiarity and soothing sense of safety and shelter it gave her.

Eli had the door half-opened when he turned back and gazed down at her. "Tell me something. Why'd you come back to the Bay?"

"I…I missed my family." *True enough. But not the whole humiliating truth.*

He angled his head, narrowed his gaze. "Uh-huh."

Obviously, he didn't believe her. He knew her too well. He knew without knowing she would have never returned if she'd had anywhere else to go. But Honey couldn't bring herself to confess she'd failed at the one career she'd wanted most in the world. She refused to admit defeat. "Will you call me when you get the autopsy report on Andy?" she pressed.

"You'll hear from me," he stepped onto the porch. "In the meantime, you might want to get someone to plug up whatever hole those critters used to get into the attic."

"Yes. Okay. I'll take care of everything first thing in the morning."

"Goodnight." Eli raised an arm in farewell as he bolted down the steps two at a time. He never looked back. Clearly, the sheriff couldn't get away from her fast enough.

Chapter 3

Following a somewhat restless night, Honey started her workday the next morning by calling and leaving a message for the critter catcher. She had questions requiring answers and her first stop once she reached town was the Blue Oyster Grill. She stepped under the crime scene tape at the Blue Oyster Grill and pressed her face against the glass front window. The restaurant was dark inside but as she turned away, she caught a shadow moving into the dining area from the back where she knew the kitchen was located. Dashing to the door, she knocked as loudly as she dared.

When no one answered, Honey knocked even louder, believing the shadowy figure might be the deceased chef's wife Thea. Andy and Thea had lived in the small apartment above the restaurant since the day the Grill opened. Two story dwellings were regarded as high rises in Blue Oyster Bay.

Just when Honey was about to give up the door opened a crack, and dull-dark brown eyes gazed out at her. Thea. The new widow appeared dazed, evidently still in shock.

"Thea, it's me, Honey Mayhew. I am so sorry for your loss. I wanted to extend my condolences." She gave a gentle push on the door. "May I come in?"

Thea opened the door wider, just enough to allow Honey entry. As soon as the door closed behind her,

Honey enveloped the new widow in a warm hug. "Is there anything I can do?"

The dark-haired woman shook her head. Honey felt Thea's body trembling before the woman pushed away from her embrace.

Chef Andy's widow wore her usual attire of a black Blue Oyster Grill tee-shirt and black baggy pants. Her short frizz of black curls appeared tangled. Not a hint of makeup touched her pale complexion.

Honey's heart went out to the clearly anguished woman. "Thea, may I sit with you for a while?"

Thea released a heavy sigh. Lowering her head, she nodded.

Honey skirted the chalk mark where Chef Andy's body had lain as she followed the grieving widow thru the scattered tables to the back of the Grill where the oyster bar and cash register were situated. As she followed Thea, she skimmed the restaurant seating area as if she'd never seen it before, as if she would find a clue to what had happened here.

Thea sank into the seat of a table for two.

Honey sat opposite. "Have the police contacted you this morning?"

Thea shook her head. "Not yet."

"I'm sure they will, as soon as Eli knows something."

Thea nodded and clasped her hands together.

She was a quiet woman, always had been. Honey studied her briefly, noting there were no tell-tale, red-rimmed eyes to signify she'd been crying all night. Still, her grief was palatable.

Honey questioned gently. "Had Andy been ill?"

"No." Thea shrugged. "He had diabetes. Nothing

new. Andy didn't pay any attention to his doctors or his diet."

"He hadn't any heart trouble?"

"No."

It wasn't Thea's inertia that bothered Honey; it was the bruises high up on her arms. Noticing Honey's stare, the widow quickly grabbed her sweater from the back of the chair and slipped into the garment, quickly concealing the faint purple bruises.

Before Honey could ask another question, the front door swung open. Carol, hostess and head server, bustled through the door, slamming it behind her. Glaring at Honey, she snapped, "What are you doing here?"

"Good morning to you, too."

Hovering over Honey, Carol jammed her fists on her plentiful hips. She was a tall, full-figured woman who flaunted a wardrobe of blue jeans and flowing, rhinestone-studded caftan tops. Perhaps seeking a bit of sparkle, she'd sprinkled multi-colored rhinestone bobby pins through her drab toast-brown hair. Emerald, sapphire, and ruby "jewels" twinkled at random. And then there was her perfume, a thick nauseatingly sweet scent which pushed Honey's allergy button.

She glowered at Honey, who was attempting to hold back a sneeze. "You're one of those fake news vultures, pouncing on a grieving woman," she hissed with contempt.

"Excuse me?" Honey'd heard the insult before. She tamped down her anger. "I came to extend my condolences."

"Yeah?"

"Yes. And to see if there was any new…news," she added quietly and calmly, unwilling to engage in a full-out confrontation. Carol's reputation in town as a bossy busybody had been well-earned. But this was neither the time nor the place to engage in a war of wills or words. "My mother wondered if the funeral services have been arranged and if you'd like the newspaper to publish the—"

"There is no news," Carol snipped, pointing a finger inches from Honey's face. "We're planning the funeral for some time next week. I'll text you. In the meantime, here's something you can print: The Grill will open by the end of the month."

"We'll be glad to," Honey nodded her assurance. "That's good news."

"Thea's gotta earn a living," Carol mumbled.

"And you? What will you be doing?"

"Same as always. I'll be helping Thea as long as she needs me." Carol gestured toward the door. "You can leave now."

"But I'd like—"

"Or I'll call the sheriff."

At present there was no worse threat. "No need to call Eli," Honey responded quickly. But before she could move there was another soft knock on the door.

She looked over her shoulder to see Donald Turner, Blue Oyster Bay's popular, and only, attorney through the glass. Carol rushed to unlock the door for him. Turner sauntered into the restaurant with the swagger of a man who considered himself of rock star significance. Dressed in his signature blue and white seer-sucker suit, the middle-aged lawyer was every inch the southern gentleman—and shark—straight out of a Tennessee Williams drama.

He nodded to Honey and raised a questioning

eyebrow to Carol.

"She was just leaving," Carol said, snatching Honey by the elbow, forcing her up and out of the chair.

"Okay. Easy! I'm going." Honey gave Carol the side-eye as the server guided her to the door.

The door slammed behind her. And locked. With one last withering look, Carol pulled the door blinds shut with a snap and turned away. Away from Honey's prying eyes. A meeting had begun with the widow of the deceased, the Grill's number one employee and the town lawyer.

Honey supposed a legal type of meeting was common when a business owner passed away unexpectedly. Curiosity fired all the neurons in her brain as she searched for the slightest opening in the blinds. If she were caught, if she lingered by the door a minute more, it would not go well for her. The self-appointed widow protector Carol would make good on her threat to call the sheriff. Thea's best friend was that obnoxious.

Honey backed off. As she made her way to the Banner, she breathed in the salty air as if it were a soothing exotic scent. The morning sun warmed her. The Bay had none of the noise, the hustle and bustle or staleness of a big city morning. Every day was a beautiful new day, one of the few pluses in her opinion of living in the old hometown.

And the people were good, good to the bone. As a whole they were kind, hardworking people. Thea was one of those and Honey wanted to help her. Perhaps she could organize a benefit to raise money for Andy's widow. Hopefully, the Grill's new sole owner was the beneficiary of a substantial life insurance.

Thea appeared weak and overwhelmed, putty in the

hands of Carol. Carol and Donald Turner were of a different breed. What was Carol advising her? What was the attorney suggesting to Thea? And why were Thea's arms bruised?

Honey would give anything to know the answers, but she'd be content for the time being by doing some research at the office.

The bell jingled as Honey opened the Banner Bay office door.

Grandma Bess looked up, seemingly startled by the bell. Miss Bess sat at her desk, eating a large cinnamon bun, sipping coffee, and chatting with her daughter-in-law, the editor.

"Good morning, Grandma Bess."

Her grandmother smiled, red glossy lips dripping with icing. "Sugha."

"Are you writing the obits this morning?" Honey asked, making a beeline for the coffee pot.

Her seventy-seven-year-old grandmother nodded. Bess Mae Mayhew spent most days in the newspaper office claiming work kept a body young. She clung to the '60's of her youth with more fervor than most who reached legal age during those years. She not only listened to the 60's music, she sang along. She knew the all the lyrics. Bess also read her horoscope daily. Her nonconformist fashion style mainly consisted of long, homemade skirts in shades of purple topped with lavender tee shirts which usually carried a message. Today she was wearing, *Make love not war.*

When her head wasn't covered by a baseball cap, Miss Bess's hair could be seen from blocks away. Honey's grandmother refused to be the stereotype of a white-haired old lady and colored her hair a bright tangerine at Bini White's beauty salon. She wore the wiry mass pulled back at the nape of her neck. A wide purple grosgrain bow held back the strays and wrapped around the bright orange tangle at her nape. Oddly enough, Grandma Bess's screaming hair shade complimented her light blue eyes and fair, deeply fluted skin.

Although she observed the rule that held a southern lady never went out into the sun without a hat, her observance began too late in life to have been much help. No one dared count the lines fanning Grandma Bess's eyes and bracketing her mouth. Still, Honey admired her attention to appearance. The eclectic senior never left the house without full paint, which included lavender eyeliner. Her trim figure was the result of power walking twenty minutes on the beach every morning.

Honey secretly hoped she'd inherited Grandma Bess's genes.

The old woman gently wiped her mouth of cinnamon crystals. "So sad about Andy. Ah'll be adding his passin' to the column."

Editor and publisher Laura Mayhew interrupted. "Miss Bess, we've been thinking about running a separate item on Andy. What do you think?"

"Ah think you should."

"Honey will write it."

"I will?"

"Thea did it, don't ja know," Bess declared, nodding sagely. "She killed him."

"What?" Honey cried in surprise.

Laura's eyes widened, color drained from her face. "What are you talking about, Momma?"

"The spouse always does it."

"No. Not in this case." Honey shook her head. "I just came from the Grill. Thea is devastated. Her pain is real."

Grandma Bess waved a gnarly, liver-spotted hand. "Ah'm guessin' that drama's for show."

"I don't think so." Unwilling to argue with her grandmother, Honey shifted her attention to her mother. "Thea is totally destroyed." Grandma Bess lowered her voice to whisper, "Rumor has it Andy had a mistress."

Honey gasped.

Her mother choked on her coffee. "What?"

"Folks at the senior center were talkin' where my band played yesterday for the potluck. That's why ah'm late with the obits. 'Sides, ah don't like to write them. More often than not these days, ah'm intimately familiar with the deceased."

"I know, Mama," Editor Laura apologized. "I'm sorry, but it's a job someone has to do."

"Ah'd rather be singing."

Grandma Bess played the piano and sang with her trio. Dave Morris played the drums and Henry Ignazio played the guitar. Honey suspected that Henry had a twenty-year crush on Miss Bess.

"Is there more to this mistress rumor?" Honey asked, perching on the edge of her grandmother's desk.

"It's not much of a rumor. Susie Block's daughter saw him walking by the bay one night a few months ago with a woman."

"Who?" A jolt of excitement shot through Honey. Maybe there actually was a story here. Jealousy! Crime of passion! A motive! "What woman?"

"Too dark to tell."

Honey let out a deflated sigh. "That's just nothing.

Nothing but hurtful gossip. The woman might have been Thea, his wife."

Honey's mother tapped her red pencil against her chin. She edited the old fashion way, printing the story and then editing the hard copy before doing the final edit on the computer. "A rumor like that might be worth looking into. Maybe Thea believed Andy was—"

"And maybe he suffered a heart attack," Honey interrupted. As much as she wanted a story, the idea of the middle-aged, overweight, self-absorbed chef being involved in an affair seemed ridiculous. And in the past, she had learned a valuable lesson about jumping the gun. "This is how vicious rumors start. Speculation. *Wild* speculation."

"You're right," her mother agreed. "Let's get to work and forget this until we have facts and know something different."

"Right." Honey agreed with her mother, but in the next moment she began to rethink her position. While Blue Oyster Bay wasn't exactly Sin City, she might just as well go ahead and investigate. No harm in that. "But if I find some spare time, I might look into the idea. We can't afford to ignore any lead if we want to sell papers."

Her mother shot her a warning look. "We don't want to create a scandal in the name of sales."

"Of course not." But Honey knew many of the surviving, even thriving, news organizations did exactly that. Creating news was hardly an original concept. But there was nothing to stop Honey from following up on the rumor after she took care of some important business.

****

Alvin Gray of the Blue Oyster Bay Critter Control Company met Honey back at the beach house. He carried a ten-foot ladder on his rusty old pickup truck. Fred warily eyed the critter-getter from his veranda doggie bed. He didn't wag his tail and quickly closed his eyes after an initial once-over of the stranger. Some watch dog she had. His protective instinct depended on his mood.

Alvin greeted Honey with a bear hug. She'd forgotten they had been high school classmates. "Hey Honey, I never thought to see you back in the Bay."

She squirmed out of the tall, lanky man's reach. His skin, appearing dark and dry as old bark, signaled a decades-long lack of sun protection. sunscreen. "I don't plan on being here for long, Alvin. I'm a professional journalist now."

"Same as me. I'm a professional now too." He pushed a hand through long, sun-streaked dirty brown hair. "I own this here critter control business."

"Congratulations are definitely in order," she said, smiling. "And if you'll just remove those raccoons from my attic quickly, I'll be really grateful."

The critter trapper's bushy brows squiggled together. "Who said you had raccoons in your attic?"

"Sheriff Gibson."

"Aaah." He nodded, flashing a knowing smile. "Yer ole flame. Always thought you two would marry up soon as you graduated from high school."

"Well, we didn't," she replied, inexplicably more irritated by his assumption than she should have been. "How long will this job take?"

"You in a rush?"

"I have to get back to the Banner."

Alvin scratched his beard. "Guess when the major leagues came callin' and swooped Eli up, it sort of put the kibosh on the marriage plans, eh?"

"Eli's plans had nothing to do with mine. I always planned to go to college." Honey really did not want to get caught up in this conversation. "And now I need raccoons removed from the attic."

"Good old Eli was the town's hero there for a while. Before he got hurt."

Before he got hurt. The words echoed in Honey's head. Eli had been her hero too. A massive amount of texts shot back and forth between her studying in Tallahassee and Eli playing ball in Texas. He'd signed with the Texas baseball team for what seemed at the time a staggering sum. But after he'd been hurt, he stayed in Texas and underwent surgery to repair the torn rotator cuff. He'd hoped to play after he'd healed. Honey had offered to fly to Texas for the surgery, but Eli insisted she stay in school. Their future suddenly became uncertain. Worse, the career-ending injury happened during her senior year when she'd been attending classes round the clock in order to graduate early to join him.

"Sad about the cuff," Alvin muttered with a wag of his head.

Sad wasn't the word. The injury changed both of their lives. They'd been too young to know how to cope. "Yes. Now about the raccoons…"

"Right, right. No sense cryin' over spilt milk, is there?" he asked, with no apparent expectation of an answer. "I'm gonna git those critters for you now." He grabbed the ladder from the back of his truck and looked back at her. "It sure would be like one of them fairy tales if you and Eli got together again, now that you're both back in town."

"I'll be leaving town soon." *She hoped.*

"Pity. Pity."

Within the hour, the critter catcher caged two large raccoons and three small babies. Fred hefted himself up and chugged his way over to the cages. The raccoons hissed and Fred barked once and backed off.

"Fred, back to bed." Honey pointed to his bed. He gazed up at her with his woeful chocolate eyes before sauntering back to his battered doggie bed.

"Anything else I can catch for you?" Alvin asked after he'd stashed the cages in his truck. "Armadillos? Field mice?"

"No, thank goodness. Racoons will be all, thanks."

"Did you hear about Chef Andy?"

"Yes. Poor man. Terrible." Story leads sometimes came from the most unlikely. "What have you heard?"

"Didn't like him. Andy was too big for his britches. He ain't gonna be missed, if you ask me."

"Really? Why is that?"

"Do you know he cheated George K. out of his rightful shrimp price for years? If George didn't give Andy the shrimp below cost, he threatened to take his shrimp business away. The shrimp competition is tough, worse than the oyster business. George K. never had a choice; the man has four kids at home to support. He gave Andy the shrimp below cost every dang day. Now, if the restaurant closes, he'll never make up for what he's lost."

"I'm sorry to hear that." More than sorry, Honey was mildly disturbed by the news. "If Thea keeps the restaurant open, she'll be fair. Thea will pay a fair price."

Honey watched the critter controller leave before heading for the docks. She needed to chat with George K as soon as his boat moored.

The pling of her phone startled Honey out of her

reverie—a text.

Sugah, ah have a line on the woman seen with Andy.
Grandma Bess was on the case.

Chapter 4

Pure adrenalin lifted Honey's feet off the ground as she raced south on Main to the Curly Q Beauty salon on Gulf Way Court. If the chef was involved in a love triangle, his sudden mysterious death might indeed be murder. A hometown homicide born from a hot love triangle was just the sort of story people loved to read.

The Curly Q Beauty Salon was one of two hair salons in town, but the Curly Q offered the usual services for rock bottom prices of ten dollars and up. Grandma Bess had a standing once-a-month appointment for routine maintenance. Waxing brows and lips and coloring her white roots to her signature brilliant orange took half a day. She normally added a few hours more to her appointment for lunch, tea, and an earful of town gossip. Miss Bess called it her glamour day.

Honey found her grand lounging in a stylist chair reading a celebrity magazine. Her hair was slathered in a pungent red rinse. Honey flashed a smile and a wave to the owner, operator, and stylist, Bini White before hurrying to her grandmother's side.

Breathing hard from both sun and speed, she all but fell into the empty dryer chair beside Miss Bess, who by a lift of her eyebrows appeared surprised to see her so soon. The Curly Q still used the old fashioned giant hooded dryers which had caught Honey off-guard on her first visit.

"Miss Bess," she said lowering her voice. "What does your text mean? You found a line on the woman. What woman?"

Bess put down her magazine, gave Honey a wink, gesturing to the back of the salon where a pitcher of sweet tea sat cooling in a bucket of ice. If Bini overheard their conversation, Honey knew it would be all over Blue Oyster Bay within the hour. Once out of earshot, her grand whispered, "Chef Andy had a mistress."

"What? Who?"

"Rachel Grover."

"The hostess at Beasly's?" Most of the locals ate at Beasly's Oyster Bar. For the most part tourists chose not to travel down the dirt road to the riverside eatery.

"Yep. Beasly's hostess."

"Grand, it's…well, it's hard to believe. Where did you hear this?"

"From the part-time hostess at the Oyster Ale Spot, Gwen Something. She was in here earlier for a wash and cut."

Honey's initial excitement popped like a pin-pricked balloon. Gwen Something was hardly a reliable source. "Ms. Something saw Andy and Rachel together?"

"Could have been business, but she told me they were holding hands. Who holds hands in a business meeting?"

Honey said it again. "Hard to believe."

"When you get right down to it, Sugah, a lot of things in life are hard to believe."

"Rachel is way younger than Andy."

"The two of 'em had a lot in common, I reckon. Hot kitchens and tiny oysters—since the Spill," she explained needlessly. "Tiny oysters."

"Uh-huh." The Gulf oil spill of 2010 damaged the oyster beds along the Gulf coast, a loss that pretty much devastated the Bay's economy. Honey felt certain that no one who lived outside of the area knew the extent and length of the hardship endured by the townspeople. For years the disastrous event had been known simply as the Spill—with a capital S. The oyster men were forced to raise their prices and lower their standards.

"You going to go see Rachel?" Bess asked, barely stopping for a breath. "'Cause ah can go with you."

An uneasiness settled in the pit of Honey's stomach. "I don't know. If I knew the official cause of Andy's death it would be one thing. But if he had a heart attack there's no sense in stirring up trouble."

"And some folks think journalists don't give a hoot."

"On the other hand, how could it hurt if I just stopped into Beasly's?"

"Couldn't."

"Since your hair is still, ah, turning, it would be so helpful if you'd stay here and keep your ears open for any more information."

Grandma Bess narrowed her eyes and lowered her voice. "Like a CI?"

"Exactly."

"I'll stay an extra hour, no problem with that." Her sparse brows folded into a frown. "Gotta look good for the funeral."

"Do you know when the funeral will be held?"

"The day after tomorrow. Heard it right here. They're moving fast on Andy, bless his heart."

"What? Has the M.E. given his okay?"

"Didn't hear about that. You think he'll find something...murderous?"

"Don't know." Honey shrugged. "But before any funeral is held, I think the sheriff has to give the final approval."

"You gonna ask Eli?"

"If he'll answer my calls."

"Don't give up on that man, Sugha."

"Giving up on Eli happened a long time ago, Grand. Don't be getting ideas."

"Not me." She looked the picture of innocence as she walked Honey to the door, which worried Honey more than anything she'd said. Her grandmother's faded black color cape dragged on the floor, swishing all the way. "And don't you worry," Miss Bess assured her. "'Til this Chef Andy mystery is solved, you and I will be a team, Sugah. My mind is still as sharp as ever."

Honey agreed, "You're sharp as a tack." She understood that despite her frequent statements to the contrary, Miss Bess worried about her fading memory more with each passing day.

After giving Grand Bess a quick kiss on the cheek and breathing in way too much of the toxic bleach fumes emanating from her grandmother's head, Honey left the salon, eager to reach Eli. She left another voice mail asking him to call her. In the meantime, she'd check out Rachel Grover.

Honey ambled down River Street toward Beasly's deep in thought. She found it difficult to consider Rachel as "the other woman." Anyone's other woman.

The thin woman rarely smiled. Shy and quiet, Rachel had been a fixture in town as the tallest woman, standing well over six feet. Honey recalled that in high school Rachel refused to date anyone under her height, which left her without a date for the senior prom and most other school events. By Honey's calculations, Andy could not have been more than five-feet-nine inches. If Rachel had been seeing the chef on the side, she must have lowered her height requirements. She'd graduated from high school two years before Honey and gone right to work at the Oyster Ale House, beginning as an oyster shucker and sometime server. Honey had no idea when.

Like most of the Bay's residents, in all likelihood Rachel's life remained basically the same from year to year. Perhaps the excitement of an affair saved her from a totally lackluster life. From Honey's point of view, standing on the docks watching shrimp boats come and go seemed boring at best.

She shook her head, shaking out a piece of gossip she just couldn't believe. Adjusting her straw hat, she turned on Main and headed down the dirt road for Beasly's Oyster Bar. Rachel and Andy? An affair?

Although Honey was aware, like most of the town residents and most assuredly his wife, the big chef enjoyed flirting. The gleam in his eye for the pretty tourists who dined in his restaurant never faded over the years. Compared to most of them, Rachel was as plain as white bread. And five times as tall.

Beasly's Oyster Bar had begun to serve early lunch when Honey arrived at her destination. Serving as hostess, Rachel greeted her with a curt nod.

Honey smiled. "Hey, Rachel. Good to see you. It's been a long time."

"I heard you were back in town."

"For a short time. How have you been?"

She gave Honey a tight smile. "Good."

"You look great, Rachel."

"Thanks." With a quick, even tighter smile, Rachel picked up a laminated menu from a slot on the wall. "Follow me."

Honey followed. Her memory of Rachel as the high school ugly duckling was in error. The hostess had obviously been reinvented as a swan. Her sharp-angled features, narrow nose, and high cheek bones gave her a model profile. Honey would kill for Rachel's strawberry-blond hair that flowed freely down her back in large glossy waves. A smudge of pink on her lips appeared to be her only makeup.

Unlike Honey's haphazard look of faded canary colored capris, tennis shoes, a Banner Bay Tee and floppy straw hat, Rachel wore a fashion forward black miniskirt and lavender halter top. Both skirt and top flaunted her figure.

Rachel stopped at a small table. "Is this okay?"

"Yes, thanks. How are the oysters today?"

"They're always fresh, always good."

"Of course," Honey said. "How long have you been working at Beasly's?"

"Four years," she replied in clipped tones. "I was at the Oyster Ale House for ten years."

Honey nodded, attempting appreciation. "A long time. You must love your work."

"I own Beasly's now."

Honey didn't hide her surprise. "Wow! Good for you. Congratulations. I had no idea you owned the business."

"I worked hard to be my own boss."

"I'd like to do a story on your success—if you're

open to that."

"No. I'm not."

"But there are only a few successful restaurants in Blue Oyster Bay. How do you manage? Have you had help?"

"Help?" Rachel's professionally arched brows gathered toward the bridge of her nose. "What do you mean? Of course I have help. Kitchen help, servers…"

"Helpful advice," Honey interrupted. "A mentor to help…like another restaurant owner? Chef Andy for instance."

Not a subtle suggestion, but Honey chose to cut to the chase. Rachel's body language telegraphed impatience. Perhaps unease?

"No mentor. No advice. I'll send over a server."

Honey had no choice but to stay and eat. She ordered a soft drink and a fried oyster basket. For the ten minutes it took her to eat, she watched Rachel. The remote but smiling hostess greeted her customers without ever looking at Honey again.

It was possible. Andy might have been having an affair with Rachel. If so, would Thea know? And if she knew, what would his beleaguered wife do? Would she kill him? What about Carol, who protected Thea as if they were sisters? How did she feel about Andy, and how he treated Thea?

Speculation. All Honey could do until the official cause of Andy's death came in from the medical examiner was speculate.

After finishing half of the oyster basket, she waved goodbye to Rachel and left. Rachel did not return the wave.

Strange relationship. She fervently whispered her

mantra despite the facts. "Puleeze. Take me back to civilization, back to a city with bright lights and normal people. Awesome people. People who don't hide in attics. Puleeze."

In big, exciting cities, she'd experienced two layoffs, or two blessings, according to her mother. Three blessings, if she counted her fiancé, Mark Bayless, breaking off their engagement shortly after she received her second blessing—the blessing of being fired from *The Weekly Spin*. She'd overheard Mark talking on his cell, sharing with his best buddy that he'd scored with a gorgeous model, a hot babe soon to join the world's most beautiful women roster. Worse, he then asked for advice on how to break up with Honey, who he went on to describe as a mediocre writer and nowhere near as good looking as his new supermodel squeeze.

In the past, eavesdropping had landed Honey leads on some interesting stories, but in this instance, the fine art of inquisitive listening had just about broken her heart. She sent Mark a break-up text before the scumbag could dump her. She took the cowardly way out knowing that if she'd attempted to end their relationship in person she would have sobbed like a child.

Mediocre! No way.

Nowhere near as gorgeous as a magazine model? Okay, she'd give him that. Honey preferred the natural look. A stroke of peach gloss on her lips—one and done. She blamed her ugly feet and long toes on her missing father, but she did have good legs. If she'd been pressed to name one attractive physical attribute she possessed, she would have said her legs...long and of a decent shape. Which Mark didn't mention.

Shaking off her physical perusal, she went back to

counting her blessings. Lastly and hugely, her fourth and final blessing came when her savings ran out. She found herself penniless and jobless in a city where the cost of living set the high-end bar for the country, perhaps the world. *What to do?*

George K's shrimp boat hadn't left the docks. Some said the shrimper was home with the flu, but others said he'd drunk too much the night before at the Oyster Ale Spot. Another dead end.

Chapter 5

The entire town turned out for Chef Andy's funeral at the Congregational Church on 5th Street, in the center of town. Of course, almost everyone had eaten at the diner at one time or another and a few good citizens now claimed to have been close friends with the rotund chef.

Honey breathed in the thick fragrance of lilies and incense scenting the small church. She'd never been inside the church before and was surprised to see three large, beautiful, and expensive, stained-glass windows on either side of the building. The high pulpit and enormous organ appeared out of place in a small-town church but certainly commanded attention. Twenty, hard heart of pine pews sat on each side of the faded carpeted middle aisle. Chef Andy's austere closed coffin took center stage in front of the sanctuary.

The Mayhew women arrived thirty minutes before the service was scheduled to start and still were assigned to a pew in the far back. Honey noted folks only put away their flip flops and shorts for weddings and funerals. As always, her mother looked elegant wearing a simple black sheath with a long strand of pearls. Cricket dressed in a long black skirt and a black and white gingham top, and Grandma Bess looked resplendent in a royal purple dress with a small purple feathered hat atop her orange hair.

"Ah never wear black to a funeral, Sugha," she whispered. "Folks just do not expect it of me. How much nicer to wear a royal, respectful color."

"You look beautiful, Grand." And she did. Miss Bess's eyes were delicately lined, and her cheeks blushed to a healthy cherry hue.

Grandma Bess eyed Honey askance. "You might have taken a little more care."

Honey knew appearances meant everything in a small town. Yet here she was, fodder for tomorrow's gossip. She tugged down on her skirt. "I was running late." Honey had snatched a black blouse and miniskirt from the closet. A skirt that didn't quite fit anymore. "Most of my clothes are still packed away."

The next sound she heard might have been Bess *tsking*.

The next movement she felt was her grand's elbow poking her in the ribs.

"Ouch. What?"

"You know we folks in the South prefer an open casket," she whispered. "That way you know the deceased is really dead."

"Grandma Bess," she hissed. "Quiet!"

Poked in the ribs, five minutes later, Honey responded with a scowl.

"Look who's a'comin'."

Honey watched as Thea walked slowly down the aisle, Carol's arm wrapped around her shoulders in support. Both women wore ankle length black dresses, but a thick black veil concealed Thea's face.

Donald Turner, wearing his usual signature seersucker garb followed behind the two women and took a place beside them in the first pew.

Rachel appeared a few minutes later, slipping into a rear pew. Honey only knew this from her grandmother's sudden grunt and another elbow in her ribs. "Rachel's hiding in the back."

"Shhh," Honey's mother hushed her with a low warning without ever moving her lips.

Cricket ventured a look over her shoulder. "Here comes Henry."

"Grand, did Henry know Andy?" Honey asked.

"No, but he knows I did, and he wanted to be here with me. To support me."

As if she needed supporting. "You have your entire family here to support you," Honey whispered. *And Henry sat on the other side of the aisle.*

"Not the same, Sugha. Henry and me, we have a special connection."

"A special, what?"

"Doesn't he look handsome?"

"Yes, he…he does." Honey agreed with her grandmother, Henry looked handsome in his dark suit, gray shirt, and darker gray tie. But her mind stuck on "special connection." Just what did Miss Bess mean?

"If only his daughter wasn't a bitch."

"Grand! Language. You're in church."

"I'll explain later."

Grandma Bess had a lot of explaining to do as far as Honey was concerned.

Eli was one of the last to arrive. Honey caught him out of the corner of her eye on one of her frequent over the shoulder reconnaissance checks. He strode in alone and slipped into the end of a rear pew. His gaze appeared focused on the coffin.

Instead of his usual sheriff's uniform, he was

55

obviously dressed in his going to church best, wearing a sports jacket, striped shirt, and navy tie. Honey sighed. The man she once loved with a fierce devotion looked like a male model in an upscale catalogue. It had been years since she'd seen him this way, handsome and absolute. She felt an odd twist of her heart, a small painful squeeze.

Eli easily stood out in the small church. There was a time when Honey would have stood proudly beside him. She meant to see him after the service but only to discover if he had more information on Chef Andy's death. He had never gotten back to her about the funeral. Leo had.

If the rotund chef had been murdered, she noted all the suspects were gathered here today to give him a respectful send-off. Honey ticked off the people she considered persons of interest: Thea, the berated wife; Carol, the beleaguered restaurant manager and close friend of the wife; Donald, the partner with perhaps a grievance, and lastly, Rachel, perhaps the jealous mistress.

Honey turned her attention to the minister who painted a picture of Chef Andy as a saint of a man. She heard sobs and sniffles and briefly wondered if she'd been wrong about Andy. Who was she to judge? She hadn't lived in here for years. And she hadn't exactly buddied up to the gregarious chef since her return.

She joined the congregation to sing the final hymn, mostly as an effort to drown out Miss Bess, who had a good heart but not a singing voice that remained on key.

"Amazing Grace, how sweet thou art..."

The pall bearers, Don Turner among the diner regulars, slowly moved Andy's coffin down the aisle and out of the church to the waiting limo.

Honey was anxious to leave the church as quickly as possible. "Momma, I want to catch Eli before he leaves."

"But Sugah," her grand objected. "Ah want you to meet Henry." The old woman did not use her indoor voice.

"I'll see him outside, Grandma."

"Chasin' after Eli is not gonna do any good. You'll see him at the Mullet Toss this weekend."

"Not chasing!" And the mullet toss was the last thing Honey would be covering. She practically ran from the church, threading her way through the crowd.

She caught up with the widow first, laying a hand on the grieving woman's arm. "Thea, I'm so sorry for your loss. If there's any way I can help—" Thea turned away, toward Carol.

"I told you once before, leave her alone," Carol warned tight-lipped.

Honey tried again. "If I can do anything—"

"Show some respect and give her space. Leave her alone."

"I can see she'd devastated, we all—"

"You don't know the half of it," Carol spat. "Andy wasn't who any of these people thought. The man left a mountain of debt and most of it he owed Don Turner. Thea has more than enough to deal with. She's overwhelmed. So now that you know, just stay out of our faces until we can get things straightened out."

Nodding, mouth opened in surprise, Honey backed away. She hadn't expected the sotto voce tirade. Nor the information which left her more confused than satisfied. A legacy of a mountain of debt! She looked up just in time to see Eli giving her the evil eye. She knew the look he used. Without saying a word, he telegraphed his disapproval for approaching the widow outside the church. She understood and flushed as shame stirred in her belly. She would not have made such a move in the days when he knew her best, when she was a journalism student. The time before her sensitivity had been beaten out of her by the rise of ambition. She lowered her head and stepped aside to wait for her family. She would speak to Eli later.

"Well, you missed Henry now," Grandma Bess huffed as she sidled up beside her. "He's goin' to the grave site with his daughter."

"I'm sorry, Miss Bess. I'll meet him soon. I promise."

At the cemetery, Honey surreptitiously searched the crowd, almost missing Rachel Grover who stood in the rear of the onlookers beneath an old oak tree. Still as a statue, the willowy woman watched. Almost shrinking into the tree, she hid behind large dark sunglasses and a wide-brimmed hat.

Donald Turner, however, was very much up-front and present. The mayoral candidate stood on one side of Thea while Carol stood on the other. They appeared to be holding up the grieving widow. Turner and Rachel, two mourners either one whom, in Honey's opinion, may have been responsible for Chef Andy's demise.

"It's a great day for a funeral," Miss Bess said, nodding her approval to no one in particular as she surveyed the grave site scene. "Sun and blue skies. Good omens."

"I still can't believe he's gone," Honey's mother commented quietly.

Cricket gave a mournful sigh. "He was the best chef

in town."

Honey was struck by a sudden thought. "Momma, if we're all here, who's manning the Banner?"

"We're closed for two hours out of respect."

Honey tamped down the shock that settled in her throat. "Newspapers don't close, news organizations operate twenty-four seven."

"We've never operated twenty-four seven." Her mother added a reminder. "This is Blue Oyster Bay."

"Right. The rules are different here. I keep forgetting." The Banner closed whenever it suited her mother. Honey didn't think she could ever get used to working for a small-town newspaper, even if she owned a small part of the Banner. Which she didn't. She didn't think. But what if she did?

Oh, she badly needed to get out of town.

But right now she wanted to chat with Rachel. She kept her eyes on the woman. When the casket began to be lowered, the secret mistress turned and walked toward the small sand and dirt parking lot. Honey started after her but had only reached the road when Eli stepped out from behind his police car parked on the side of the road.

"Where are you headed?"

Caught off guard, she hedged. "I…I thought I might speak to Rachel for a minute. Or maybe I'll just head back to the office."

"Head back to the office. That's the right choice. Leave these people alone. You're not working for me. And you're not a licensed investigator. So don't get in their way or mine. You don't even belong in the Bay."

For whatever reason, Eli saying she didn't belong in his—and her—hometown, stung. "Of course I do. I have as much right to be in Blue Oyster Bay, and to be in this cemetery as you do."

"I'm serious. I'll lock you up on obstruction if I have to."

He was threatening her with jail?

"You cannot intimidate me, Eli. This is a free country with a free press. My rights are protected."

"From what I heard, you carried your rights too far and got yourself in trouble at your last job."

How did he know about that?

"It was a misunderstanding."

"Who gets fired from a tabloid? A rag?"

"The Spin is not a rag."

"And, as I know firsthand, you're as patient as the day is long." Anger flashed in his eyes. Oddly, Honey found the dangerous glint a new and attractive element to the man. But his words wounded, roiling around in the bottom of her belly.

Eli knew her too well. But she knew *him* well, too. Honey changed tactics. "You know, if you weren't so stubborn, we could work together and get to the bottom of this in no time."

His eyebrows hiked to their uppermost limit. "Are you out of your mind?"

"Think about it, Eli."

In the past they had achieved great solutions together. Except for the one, she admitted silently. There had been one major problem that had separated them and brought them to today and this impasse.

"Did you hear nothing I just said?" Eli shook his head. "Thinking about working with you gives me the heebie-jeebies. We will not be working together. Now or ever. And if I see you near any of the folks who are or might be involved in Andy's death, I'll haul you to the slammer. I swear."

"I'm not a criminal." But then, she had broken his heart.

The tense silence was worse than the heated exchange.

"You can tell me," she said softly, "or I'll ask the medical examiner. Do you know the cause of death?"

"Poison."

"Poison?" she repeated.

Poison. The word, the cause, settled in her mind. Chef Andy had been murdered. She'd not really believed it. Now question upon question spun through Honey's head. What sort of poison had been used? More importantly, who used it to kill? Everyone knew poison was a woman's choice to kill. What type of poison might have been kept in the Blue Oyster kitchen? Where else could he have had access?

"Poison kills slowly," she murmured. "Usually. What type of poison?"

Eli's frown deepened. "That's all I know right now and all you're going to hear from me," he said. "Now, go. And stay out of my investigation. Are we clear?"

"Clear." She couldn't count on Eli's cooperation. No surprise. He was the law in the Bay, which made him the Big Fish in their small town. Sadly, he remained just as arrogant as when he'd been king of the mound on his baseball teams. Stubborn too. He'd always been stubborn. But in the past she'd been able to wiggle her way around his bullheadedness. In some ways, in that way, they were alike.

Outwardly stiff lipped, Honey nodded solemnly. Inside, a Ferris wheel of excitement careened through her body. A story in her own hometown. A mystery to solve. A murderer to bring to justice. And perhaps a new path to success where she'd least expected to find one.

Eli shot her a warning frown before he turned and strode after Rachel.

There truly had been a murder at the Blue Oyster Grill! More than ever, Honey was determined to find the answers. She would find a way to interview Rachel without Eli being aware. Rachel was a woman perfectly capable of poisoning anyone who had crossed her. Honey felt it in her gut. She watched as the sheriff headed after Rachel. Eli, a man she had loved, a man she respected, but a man she wasn't certain could ever trust her again.

With a mystery to be solved and a murderer to be caught, Honey prepared to settle in. Before returning home, she ventured into the supermarket to do some serious grocery shopping. She also realized an update in her hot weather wardrobe would be a plus the first chance she got. Perhaps she should stop procrastinating too and unpack at least one more of her boxes. Eli's puzzled, slightly disapproving expression on seeing the piles of boxes when he was in the house served as motivation enough. Honey planned a busy night. She could always repack. She'd had practice at packing.

Thirty minutes later, Honey was greeted by Fred with a wag of his tail and a full body quiver, most likely brought on by the fact she carried two grocery bags.

The ring of her cell phone startled her. Could it be Eli? But no, the screen flashed the name of her old friend from high school days and sometime co-conspirator. She answered with a snappy greeting. "Hey there, Marylu."

"Hey, Honey," Marylu spoke in a slow southern drawl. "How you doin'?"

"Fine, fine." Better now that she had a real story to investigate. "How 'bout you?"

"Ah was workin' and couldn't go to Chef Andy's funeral." She sounded pitiful. Grandma Bess was right. Southerners as a whole loved a good funeral. "Did you go, Honey?"

Marylu worked as a nurse in the Blue Oyster Bay Hospital, a small twelve-bed facility which operated more like a holding care center. Anyone seriously ill or injured was air-lifted to Mobile or Tallahassee as soon as possible. The hospital building also housed the medical examiner and the coroner. Other than Grandma Bess, Marylu had been Honey's main source for trauma information and general gossip since she'd returned.

"I did," she said. "Andy would have been proud of how many came to pay their respects."

"Bless his heart." Marylu paused for a half a second. "Do you think Thea will keep the Grill open?"

"It's too soon to tell. Maybe."

"Ah hope so. It's one of the best places to eat in town."

"You're right," Honey agreed. "Has there been any activity around the hospital today?"

"No. Not that ah noticed. Listen, are you going to the Mullet Toss this weekend?"

From murder to mullets. From funerals to fun times. Honey marveled at how quickly the people in her hometown moved on. "Yes, I think I have to cover it."

Marylu answered in a reverent tone. "It's a tradition."

Of course it was. There had always been a mullet toss. No matter what. Hurricanes could not stop a mullet toss. "I'm sure I'll have to cover it."

"Let's go together. Ah'll cover it with you. Everyone in town will be there and you might need my help figuring out who is who."

"Awesome."

"Great! Ah'll see you Saturday."

Honey breathed a sigh of relief. She would not have to attend the free-for-all event with her momma and Grandma Bess. They were dangerous together, skilled world-class manipulators who operated a joint secret plan for her future which included marriage, children, and a home in Blue Oyster Bay as soon as possible. Not that Honey was paranoid.

Marylu possessed a good heart and an inquiring mind. In high school, Honey and Marylu had been BFF's. After graduation they'd chosen different paths. Marylu attended nursing school before returning to the Bay. She worked hard and loved her hometown. She also loved just about all the single men. At only twenty-five years old, the box redhead had been married and divorced twice. Honey gave her friend credit for not giving up on love.

****

After dinner, Honey took Fred for a walk on the beach.

The Gulf breeze blew soft and warm and salty. Her toes sank into the warm sand, and a crescent moon punctuated the night sky. None of the cities she'd lived in could compare with the comfort of a beach walk, night, or day. She had to give props to Blue Oyster Bay for the unfettered sweep of clean sand and a clear sky that seemed always to be blue. And she had to admit to feeling peaceful—at the moment.

She had a home, a friend, a job, and a story. A story

that just might take her out of the Bay for good. Tonight she would be at her computer researching poisons. By tomorrow she would know everything possible about poisons…and perhaps the type of people who use them. Coming one step closer to Chef Andy's killer. Honey was on a mission. There was a killer on the loose in Blue Oyster Bay.

Chapter 6

The Bay's Annual Mullet Toss held on the island, honored the man, woman, or child who could toss a small, slippery mullet the farthest on the white sand beach. Mullets were mainly used as bait by fishermen and so were expendable. The toss attracted residents, tourists and those who made a special trip for the unique event.

Honey had witnessed enough Mullet Tosses in her lifetime. She would have been happy to stay home and write the odd event from memory.

The sun blazed overhead, promising a good turnout for the Mullet Toss. Honey quickly showered and dressed, choosing a pair of cutoff jean shorts, a faded pink Forgotten Coast T-shirt and flip-flops. She dressed for comfort, knowing she faced the possibility of a long day under the scorching sun. After slathering sunscreen on every inch of her exposed body, she pulled back her untamable mass of hair into a ponytail, put on her new supermarket beach hat and felt good to go.

"Come on, Fred. I won't leave you alone today."

She found Cricket waiting for her at the Banner Bay offices along with Marylu. Cricket had been assigned to shoot Mullet Toss pictures for the next issue of the *Bay Banner* and she immediately insisted on driving her straw-yellow, dented and dinged wreck of a car. Fred settled in the front seat next to Cricket, and Honey, feeling a bit crunched, sat in the back with Marylu.

Just four miles over the newest bridge in the area, constructed just twenty years ago, they arrived on the Island. Honey wasn't surprised to see a crowd already gathered on the beach in front of the Blue Heron Bar and Grill, perennial site of the Mullet Toss. The popular restaurant's outdoor area extended onto the white sand beach, offering a breathtaking view of the Gulf.

"Let's just wander down the beach to see who's here," Cricket suggested. "I'll take pictures of the hot guys."

"You can count the hot guys in town on one hand," Marylu said. Her droll reply spoke of experience.

"But there's some new eye candy tourists on the Island," Cricket insisted. "I've seen them in town. Keep your eyes open. They'll be here."

Honey had no interest in eye candy. After they'd walked a fair stretch neither she nor MaryLu had seen any. Given her track record, loving and losing twice, she realized happiness for her would come with professional success rather than romance. She did not need a man to make her feel validated.

However, when she spotted Donald Turner up ahead, she thought he was one man in Blue Oyster Bay who might very well be a help to her professionally. "Donald!" She waved an arm in his direction.

Cricket slid Honey the evil eye. "Sis, I'm back to the Heron."

"Uh-oh. You're on your own with that one," Marylu asserted and abandoned Honey too.

Turner approached with a wide insincere smile. He seemed oddly out of place on the beach, barefoot but wearing his signature seersucker suit and a wide-brimmed Panama straw hat. He frowned down on Fred as if he'd spotted a tick but tipped his hat to Honey. "Are you tossin' mullet or pryin' today, Honey darlin'?"

"I don't pry. I'm a reporter."

"Ah understand one hundred dollars goes to the winner."

Turner's charming southern drawl did not disguise the inference. "I'm not interested in winning contests," she told him with a smile. "Are you tossing?"

He had the grace to grin. "No, Ah'm distributing my flyers." He offered a pamphlet to her. "Ah'm running for mayor, you know."

"Yes, I heard." Honey glanced at the pamphlet photo of the smiling mayoral candidate. The twinkle in his eye looked more lecherous than friendly. She raised her gaze. Designer sunglasses concealed Turner's eyes and anything she might read in them. "The last time I saw you, Donald, you were in the Blue Oyster Grill, but I don't remember you mentioning a political run."

"Dear lady, it was not the proper time. Ah was at the Grill to pay my respects to Thea and to remind the grieving widow that ah was there for her. After all, Andy and ah were partners."

"I might have heard that too." Fred plopped down on the sand. Honey felt a difficult dog bath coming on.

"Ah've been a silent partner mostly," the candidate explained. "When Andy arrived in town from New Orleans, he had the culinary skills and reputation but not quite enough cash to open the Grill and keep it going through the startup year."

"So you stepped in and helped financially?"

"Ah invested in what ah believed to be a viable business, a five-star dining establishment sorely needed in our community."

Five-star? "Apparently you made a good investment."

"Ah like to think so."

"How will his death impact your investment?"

"My darlin,' Honey, you realize that is an impertinent question."

Fred emitted a low growl.

"I apologize, but that's what I do when investigating a story. Sometimes I have to ask questions that might seem…insensitive to you."

"Apology accepted."

"It's difficult to believe Andy is gone."

"Indeed."

"Have you heard any rumors? I mean, about another woman in his life?"

"Dear girl!"

She sighed. "I know. Rumors."

"Andy had a mistress."

"What?" Honey was caught off guard by the abrupt statement from the attorney. A statement she hadn't expected.

"Ah do know that for a fact rather than ah rumor. A beautiful, sad young woman."

"Rachel Grover?"

He nodded. "Her mama had a rovin' eye and her papa had a real bad temper. The poor girl was bound to end up in a predicament of some sort."

"Did Thea know Andy was cheating on her?"

The lawyer lowered his head and dropped his tone to a conspiratorial level. "Ah do not know. The thing is Andy broke it off with Rachel a week or so ago. At least that's what he told me."

"Did he tell you how she reacted?"

"Unhappily," he cleared his throat excessively, "Ah believe she threatened to cut off his, uh, private parts."

"Oh, wow." Honey hiked a brow. "Sounds like Rachel was very angry."

"Ah'd say so."

Honey made a mental note to look into just what an angry Rachel might do. "What about you, Donald? Did you have a good relationship with Andy?"

"Let's just say my role as silent partner had begun to be profitable until he stopped paying me for the past four months."

The loquacious mayoral candidate had more information than she would have guessed. And he was willing to share. Honey pressed on. "Had the Blue Oyster Grill profits fallen off?"

"No. Andy was spending mah money on his mistress."

"You must have been angry."

Donald's grin grew wider. "I don't get angry, darlin.' I get even."

"Oh?"

"Andy understood what would happen if he didn't get his act together."

"What would that be?" she asked.

"Ah would own the Blue Oyster Grill, of course."

"Oh." Turner's bluntness threw Honey off-guard once again. She recovered quickly. "So, do you own the Grill now, or are you Thea's partner?"

"Let's say, ah'm Thea's partner. Ah'll do right by her, you know."

Honey ignored his smarmy smile. "Do you know how she's doing? Emotionally, I mean."

"As well as can be expected." He nodded as if agreeing with himself. "Dear girl, Ah've been extremely patient with you but ah do have campaigning to do."

"I appreciate your time." Honey's inherited dog struggled to his feet. She tightened his leash. "One last question, will the Grill open again soon?"

"Of course, in due time." He placed a hand on her shoulder. "Ah have to be moving along. As ah distribute my flyers, ah'm counting on each great citizen of the Bay to reward me with a vote." He withdrew his hand and lowered his voice as if he were imparting a top government secret. "Ah'm expecting a tough campaign this year."

"Good luck, then." She watched as he turned into a family picnic. Donald Turner would be the last person to get her vote. For all she knew he might be the killer. He had reason, motive. Honey's spontaneous interview with the mayoral candidate had proved more informative than she'd expected. She wouldn't put it past the lawyer to push out Thea and take over the Grill.

Honey's mind raced with possibilities as she rushed to catch up with her sister and Marylu.

"What was that all about?" Cricket asked.

"Seems Donald Turner was Andy's silent partner."

Marylu gasped. "What? Oh, my gosh. Do you think he was an unhappy partner, who, like, killed Chef Andy?"

Honey shrugged. "It's possible, I guess. At least it's something to look into. I think our readers should know a partnership existed."

Cricket elbowed Honey. "Over there, there's the sheriff."

At the word sheriff, Honey's mind went from full

speed Donald Turner down to zero and blank. She spotted Eli among the crowd watching the Mullet Toss. Her heart beat a bit faster. She drew a deep breath. Tall and commanding, with his arms crossed and feet planted in the sand, he owned the crowd and the toss. "I need to talk with him."

Marylu shot a knowing grin. "Ah'll bet you do."

"About Andy."

Cricket pulled up the camera around her neck. "Okay. I'm going to snap some mullet shots."

"I'll join you in a minute."

"And I'll be in the bar having an adult beverage," Marylu put in.

"I'll have one of those too. I'll find you," Honey said and started toward where Eli stood. Until Fred sank to the sand. "No. Not now, Fred. Just a few more yards and you can take a nap."

The dog looked up at her. His tongue lolled from the side of his mouth.

"Come on…up. Up." Unable to move the bulldog, she waved to Eli but clearly his attention was fixed on the little boy attempting to toss a slippery mullet—or on the caller. He brought his cell phone from his pocket and pressed it against his ear. Instead of his sheriff's uniform, he wore a tee shirt and khaki cargo shorts. Flip-flops on his feet, sunglasses and a baseball cap shaded his face from the sun. Her heart gave a little leap.

Honey watched as the little mullet fish kept sliding from the frustrated little boy's hand. They were slippery little fish. If she could get over to the child, she'd help him. But the more she tugged at Fred's leash, the more the bulldog dug in his heels, refusing to move.

Eli ended his call. He crouched down on his heels to

help the frustrated youngster hold onto his fish. Before she could blink, the little mullet landed a respectable distance in the sand. The grinning sheriff high-fived the laughing child and stood. He was about to leave without seeing her.

Feeling desperate, Honey shouted. "Eli!" Something no well-bred southern woman should do. Yet she did yell again, "Eli!"

His head swung in her direction. She motioned for him to come to her side. He didn't immediately respond, but after a moment he slowly sauntered in her direction. The sexy stubble on his jaw became noticeable as he stopped at her side. "Morning." He cocked his head in what she could only describe as warily. "What can I do for you?"

He stood close enough for Honey to smell the scent of coconut sunscreen, close enough for her to feel dwarfed by his height and intimidated by the breadth of his shoulders. She became more physically aware of him each day. Why was that?

"Are you here to toss?" she asked, a harmless question meant to be friendly and casual. And to put him at ease.

"No, the sponsors think I have an advantage with my arm, although I haven't pitched in eight years. What's up?"

"I just wondered if you'd heard anything more about Chef Andy."

"No." He shook his head. "And as I said, as I'd hope to make clear, I won't be sharing anything I do hear with you."

"But I've learned a few things about Andy that I'll share with you."

"Yeah?"

"Andy had a girlfriend and a silent partner. Did you know?"

"I'll tell you what I know." Eli pushed his sunglasses to the top of his head. To Honey's chagrin, anger flashed in his eyes. "I've seen enough of journalists creating the news. It's not going to happen here." He turned to leave. "Do you understand me?"

"Wait!" She yanked on Fred's leash, and this time by some miracle the dog got up. She marched after Eli, kicking up sand with every step. "No, I'm not trying to make something of nothing. I hope it's nothing...I...I just thought I'd share what I just learned with you."

He stopped. Faced her. Tight-lipped. "I don't need your help. I've warned you, I'll put you behind bars if I have to. Now I'm begging. Please. Don't. Help. Me."

Her apology died on Honey's lips.

"Eli...I wondered where you ran off to." A tall, willowy blond sidled up to the sheriff. Slipping her hand in his, the beauty turned to Honey. "Hello."

"Hello." Honey forced a smile. The bronzed woman was all legs and cleavage and glossy scarlet lips.

The glossy lips responded, "I'm Krystal Warren. So nice to meet you."

"Honey Mayhew." She dipped her head in greeting as the pit of her stomach lurched and fell. Eli's girl was cover model caliber complete with big brown eyes. Beneath her filmy beach cover-up, Krystal's plentiful curves were on full display in a white barely-there bikini.

"So pleased to meet you," the blond cooed, foregoing eye-contact with Honey. "And so sorry we must run off." Sliding on her designer sunglasses, she quickly dismissed Honey. Slanting a warm smile to the silent sheriff, Krystal gave a slight pull on his hand. "My parents are waiting, Eli."

He nodded, his gaze still on Honey. She read the warning in his eyes and nodded in reply. In the past they'd become quite skilled in unspoken communication. He'd been afraid Honey was about to upset his new love. And as much as the zing in her belly urged her not to let this opportunity pass without at least a sarcastic remark, she held her tongue and returned the phony smile.

"Sweetie, let's go."

Eli, also apparently known as Sweetie, gave way to Krystal.

Honey's heart leaped into a runaway rhythm as she watched him stride away holding hands with his new love. Krystal was everything Honey was not, languid grace and sophistication. Eli deserved love, a woman totally devoted to him. And yet Honey's heart threatened to explode.

Eli was about to meet Krystal Warren's parents. A move that sounded serious. Any hope Honey might have entertained of reuniting with Eli, despite her protestations, dissolved like so much spun sugar left in the sun.

"Are you okay?" Marylu rushed up to Honey's side.

"Sure. Eli and me..." She wet her lips. "We were over years ago."

Years ago.

"Is that your cell?"

"Oh." Honey tore her gaze away from the handsome couple strolling down the beach toward the restaurant and answered her phone. Her mother calling to make certain she and Cricket were covering "the Toss."

After assuring the worried editor and publisher, Honey pulled Fred through the sand until she and Marylu caught up with Cricket, who was still taking photos of contestants at the Mullet Toss site. Honey was more than ready to leave. She didn't want to risk running into Eli and his new love again. Just the thought hit her like a blow to her stomach.

"Cricket, it's hotter than the devil's furnace. Do you have enough pictures?"

"You bet."

"Ready, Marylu?"

"Oh, yeaah."

"Good. Let's go," Honey coaxed. "When you've seen one Mullet Toss, you've seen them all."

The looks Cricket and Marylu exchanged told her everything she needed to know. They assumed Honey had been upset by seeing Eli with someone new. Well, they might be right. Though she hadn't expected her reaction. She wasn't a jealous person. Even if she had a reason to be jealous. Which she didn't.

On the return to town, she persuaded them to have lunch with her at the Blue Oyster Grill. It would have been a grand plan if the Grill had been open. But as Honey suspected, the closed sign still hung on the Grill front door. It was way too soon. They settled for a salad at the Shrimp Shack with Cricket not so subtly feeding Fred under the table. Impatient, Honey left as soon as she could, dragging a panting Fred to the Banner office to file the Mullet Toss story. She'd write it later, when she felt more objective. Soon after Cricket followed her into the office and began to upload her photos.

"Look, I got one of Eli and his girlfriend."

"What?"

"Check your email."

Against her better judgement, Honey opened the mail. It was like a car wreck you could not *not* watch. Her heart plummeted to her toes. Curled toes. A dry lump settled in her throat as she stared at the picture of a striking, smiling Eli and his beautiful girlfriend. But not for a minute would she allow Cricket to think she cared. "Nice!" she enthused in her chipper voice. "Great photo!"

She heard Cricket sigh.

She hit the delete button.

Thirty minutes later, on the pretext of having to go home and unpack her boxes, she left the office.

Yes, Honey hurt, *had* hurt, because she blamed herself for bringing the heartache to Eli and to herself. She should have done what he asked and waited for him to be ready again. They'd had a pact. Two years behind him, she had to finish college. He would use the time to begin his career. They dreamed of his being picked up by a winning team—and he was. But then the dream ended. Eli suffered a shoulder injury. She offered to fly to Chicago and help with his recovery. He put her off. Asked her to wait until they had a clear idea of the future after surgery and therapy. He had promised her a good life, a secure financial future and suddenly his promises meant nothing. He told her, he begged her, to wait until he straightened out the bad hand fate had delivered. But he was a procrastinator, and she was impatient.

Honey refused to wait any longer. She'd graduated. It was time to start her life; if he was locked in inertia, unwilling to move forward, she was not. She told Eli she would always love him, and he would always know where to find her.

His response was to join the Navy.

Six years later, reflecting over her rush to begin a new life, life as an adult, she realized she'd been impulsive. She'd been immature, and so had he. Both of them had been too proud to start over with new dreams. Could have, would have, should have.

Honey didn't open any boxes when she got home. Not one. She opened her laptop and settled in a deck chair to let the new information stew. It was her process, her path to finding answers. She barely paid attention to the warmth of the sun, the scent of salty air, nor the waves lapping on the beach as the tide rolled in. Fully concentrating, Honey made an outline of the murder, the time, place, and the possible suspects.

Oddly enough, her best ideas came when she was in a relaxed mode. She grabbed her fishing pole, whistled for Fred to follow her, and sauntered down the beach to fish. She'd had no epiphany as she reeled in her line and cast it out again. No answer came to mind. Who had done it? And why?

Thea, Andy's wife, was in the best position to do him in. But why? Did she know about Rachel? Did jealousy drive her to murder? Chef Andy's outgoing personality was the reason folks dined at the Blue Oyster Grill. Without him, would Thea be able to earn a living?

Perhaps the mistress offed him. Had glamorous Rachel been waiting for the chef to leave his plain, shy wife? When he hadn't, her subsequent anger drove her into a fit of passion. Honey also considered Andy's silent partner. Was Donald Turner angry enough over Andy's skimming money to kill his partner? Of course, if it had been public knowledge about the roaches, some irate, slightly deranged diner might have decided to kill the chef. Honey's brain started to buzz. Everyone who lived in Blue Oyster Bay knew Chef Andy. There might be more than the obvious suspects. But those folks are where she needed to start to eliminate.

After an hour, she'd received not one tug on her line. No fish. She'd come up empty with neither the name of a killer or a grouper for dinner. She retreated to the veranda.

One thing for certain. She wasn't going to rush to judgement on this story. She would tamp down her impatience and wait until she had all the facts. A glass of wine and a rocking chair would do fine for now.

Watching the splash of orange and gold sunset, Honey sipped cheap red wine from a mason jar that once held Grandma Bess's homemade strawberry jam. Rocking in a weathered chair, she scanned the horizon looking over the Gulf. Fred, drooling but sleeping, nestled at her feet.

Soon stars twinkled on and off in the pitch horizon; the lights of freighter ships and tankers sparkled like fireflies. Without warning, unexpected tears streamed down her cheeks, warm and silent. She had never felt so lonely, so empty, so much a hollowed-out human.

But alone was okay, she told herself, wiping her tears away. Where had *they* come from? Alone was better. Alone, she could totally dedicate herself to the story, to solving the mystery of who killed Andy. She could freelance the story, and hopefully regain her reputation as a first-rate reporter. She could leave Blue Oyster Bay forever.

****

Honey was still sleeping the next morning when her cell rang. "Hello."

A whisper, sandpaper hoarse, male, and deep. "A body's been found in the bay."

Honey jumped up in bed. "What? When? Who is this?"

"By Blue Oyster Ale House." The caller definitely was making an effort to disguise his voice.

She recognized him anyway. Leo.

"The ME is on his way. Thought you'd like to know."

"A floater?" she questioned, uncertain whether she might still be dreaming. But only a dial tone answered her at the other end. Bolting out of bed, stomach churning and head spinning, Honey dressed in seconds. Could it possibly be another murder?

Chapter 7

The ME's old van moved slowly. Honey sped her trusty red scooter at its top speed with no traffic to maneuver this early in the morning. If she was lucky, she might beat Sam to the scene.

Patience, patience.

With half a mile to go, Honey came up just behind the Medical Examiner's van. But he'd left her no room to pass. *Patience, she repeated beneath her breath.*

Patience should be her mantra. Patience was a lesson she really needed to learn in this lifetime. Impatience had only brought trouble. Constantly and consistently.

She remembered Mark, her fickle ex, shouting. "If you weren't so freaking impatient, you never would have pushed that story to print without a complete fact check."

And then Eli's voice faint and hesitant from far away on a phone call long ago. "We have to be patient. We have to wait. I can't make any moves, career or…well, I can't make any decisions until I know if this shoulder will heal. Please understand, Honey. We can't make any plans until we know if I'll be able to play ball again."

But she hadn't waited. Not on the fact check, not on the man. She'd moved on. She'd had absolute trust in her story source, never dreaming the woman would betray her. And Honey hadn't needed to know if Eli would play ball again. She loved him and had been confident they would make whatever future they could carve work. But she suspected Eli just didn't want her anymore and his injury was a convenient way of ending their relationship. A big city ball player with a huge worshiping fan following didn't need his old high school sweetheart. Honey's determination to build her own huge fan following was born that day.

Yet, here she was, following a broken-down county vehicle along a two-lane country highway. Not the scenario of her dreams.

The van pulled up behind the restaurant to park beside the sheriff's SUV. Honey pulled into a gap between the two, jumped off her scooter, and approached the ME as he got out of the van. "Sam, what's happened?" Sam Smith had been a year ahead of her in high school.

Shielding his eyes with a sun-leathered hand, he nodded to Honey. "One of the oyster guys keeled over while he was tonging this morning. Poor fella fell into the bay and drowned. Had a little too much to drink for breakfast, I expect. Gilly supplied oysters to the Blue Oyster Grill occasionally."

"Oh, wow. I'm sorry to hear that. I never considered tonging to be dangerous. Is that why the sheriff is here?"

"Yep."

"If you learn anything that connects the drowning to Chef Andy, would you give me a call."

"I'll do my best. In the meantime, stay out of trouble."

"Why would you say that?"

"Remember back in high school when you wanted to get the story on the football player who might have been taking drugs?"

"Noooo." *She'd never admit to it. Never.*

"Ah do. You were reportin' for the school newspaper. You snuck into the locker room to eavesdrop, and the coach caught you." Sam laughed, a sniggery sort of sound. His belly shook. "You were on suspension for sixty days."

"I don't remember anything like that happening," she lied.

"And then Eli broke up with you for eavesdropping on his friends."

"I apologized and he forgave me," she said, her voice barely above a whisper.

"The way I remember it, you were dateless for six weeks at least."

"He forgave me… eventually." Eli had known how to hold a grudge.

"Honey, I gotta go. I'll let you know whatever ah hear that's legal to share."

"Thanks… Appreciate it." Honey again wondered why folks who had been lucky enough to escape the town had returned. Sam Smith was one of those who had returned. Portly and bald now but an excellent memory.

With Eli tied up, Honey had more than enough time to have another chat with Don Turner.

But as she was about to pull out of her parking space, the second sheriff's SUV pulled up behind her. Leo was at the wheel. She jumped off her scooter to stand in his path.

"What are you doing here, Honey?" Feigning curiosity, his forehead wrinkled into a five-layer frown. "It's not Miss Bess, is it?"

"Oh, no. Grandma Bess's fine." *I'm here because you called about another dead body.*

"I worry about her," he said shaking his head. "Yes, I do."

"Not to worry, she's seventy-seven years and still going strong." Honey told him. She took a fair amount of pride in her grandmother, the woman who made her crazy on a regular basis. And since Leo couldn't know Eli had warned her away from the murder investigation, she continued the conversation, asking, "Is there anything new in Chef Andy's case?"

"Don't think so."

She lowered her voice, attempting to sound menacing. "Leo, you called me out here. As it turns out, for nothing. So give me something. Do we know the type of poison used to kill him?"

Leo turned a deep shade of embarrassment pink, which had nothing to do with the sun. "Don't know if the poison thing is public information," he said, scratching behind his ear.

Honey softened her stance. "Leo, you can tell me. Off the record."

"I, I don't know," he wheedled.

She didn't need to print the information right away, but knowing the type of poison would help her investigation. "I do," she assured him. "You can trust me."

"Arsenic. Arsenic killed Andy."

Honey sucked in a breath. She knew from her research that arsenic was one of the most popular poisons among killers. Especially women. "Any suspects?"

"Eli hasn't said."

"I understand." Eli might suspect Leo would share any information related to his investigation with Honey. In which case, he would be more close-mouthed with his deputy than normal. "Who do you think the people of interest are, Leo?"

"Well, maybe Thea, for one."

Honey nodded. The spouse was always a suspect. But she could not credit sweet Thea cooking with arsenic. Although…

"And then there's Ace Barone? Do you know him?"

The name did not conjure a face, but it seemed vaguely familiar. "I think so…I might have seen him at the Blue Oyster."

"Ace worked as a part-time cook until Andy fired him a couple of weeks ago. The guy hasn't worked since, and he's been bad-mouthing Andy nonstop. We're taking a close look at him."

"Anyone else come to mind?"

Lowering his eyes, he removed his cap and sliced a hand through his hair. "Probably said too much already."

"My lips are sealed." Honey gave him a reassuring smile. "Thank you. You know, Eli's lucky to have you on his…team."

The deputy shrugged.

"Take care, Leo."

The deputy turned and headed toward the hospital emergency entrance and Honey headed back to the Banner Bay to add the latest bit of information to her story line and dig up whatever research was available on Ace Barone. If ever there was a motive for murder, money topped the list. Missing money. Owed money. Money to be made. Profits.

But had Thea known about her husband's affair with Rachel? Rachel, another woman who could so easily sprinkle arsenic into whatever she was feeding Andy.

While Don Turner appeared stoic about his share of

the profits being cut, when he first learned of the theft had he been angry enough to commit murder? And then frame Thea? With both Andy and Thea out of the picture, the biggest money-maker in town, the Blue Oyster Grill, would be his.

Thea had the motive of the affair and unknown opportunities to poison her husband. Love and revenge came close to money as a motive for murder. If Thea felt betrayed and nursed a broken heart, perhaps she'd decided to off her two-timing husband and gain sole ownership of the restaurant. And what part if any did her BFF Carol play?

Since Andy's death the women appeared joined at the hip. Carol projected the image of a good friend, confidant, and protector of Thea. Or was it all a role? Was Carol, the obviously stronger and angrier woman of the two, scheming to take over the restaurant? It wasn't far-fetched for Honey to think the manager could become the new co-owner of the Grill with little or no effort. There was little doubt in Honey's mind. Carol was clever. Had she known about Don being Andy's silent partner?

Where could a person buy arsenic in the Bay? Who kept the poison and what did they use if for, if not to kill?

So many questions. No answers. Just confusion.

"Where have you been?" her mother demanded as soon as Honey walked through the *Bay Banner* door. By the tight downward curve of her mother's lips, Honey realized Laura was deep in the role of angry editor and publisher of the *Bay Banner*.

"I've been following up on the Chef Andy murder. Did you know he was poisoned?" She paused for impact. "His death has become an official murder investigation."

"I heard. I have my own sources. And I'm shocked."

"If Eli hadn't insisted on an autopsy, everyone would have accepted Andy had a heart attack."

Her mother sank back in her chair. "Why anyone would want to kill that poor, sweet man, I don't know."

"Live roaches lived in his kitchen," Cricket explained from her computer desk across the room.

Laura Mayhew cast a withering glance her younger daughter's way. "As far as I could tell, Andy worked hard, he served good food, and he always had a friendly wave and a kind word for folks."

"The typical jolly fat chef," Honey added.

"You won't be as judgmental as you get older. At least I hope not. And don't let that attitude creep into your story."

"Of course not! Momma, from what I'm discovering about Andy—"

"Can't you just let the poor man lie in peace?"

"No. Not when someone may get away with murder. Do you want a murderer walking around town?"

"You're speculating. We only print facts."

"Momma, this is the biggest story in the Bay since the oil spill of 2010."

"Listen to me, Honey, it will not be the only story in the paper on Wednesday."

Honey waited while her mother paused to remove her glasses and wipe the lenses. "Your sister took some great pictures at the Mullet Toss. I'd like you to write that story first."

Stifling an outraged reply, Honey groaned inwardly before attempting to sway her mother with her own excitement. "I'm really on a roll with the Andy story. I have some promising leads too. More than one person in this town is not sorry the man is dead.

"Once again. This paper will not print your so-called leads. We will only print what Sheriff Gibson gives us as official information."

"I understand. But…"

"What?"

"Does Eli have to give approval to my stories before we go to print? Do you have some sort of arrangement with Eli?"

"No. This newspaper has never been involved in any sort of censorship," she huffed.

Honey had no doubt that if her mother lacked just one ounce of integrity she would collaborate with Eli. Laura loved the sheriff, had loved him when he played ball. She didn't hide her disappointment from Honey when she learned he would not be joining the family. It took months for Honey to regain her mother's full favor.

Cricket took the tense moment of silence to call to Honey. "Take your mind off the murder for a minute. The Mullet Toss photos are in the computer. You're going to have a hard time choosing which one to use."

"You can use more than one for goodness' sake. Use as many as you wish. People love to see their pictures in the newspaper."

Honey nodded to her mother and dutifully sat down at her computer. She turned it on.

"The pictures are under Mullet…"

"Thank you, Cricket. I can find them. Why are you here today if you don't mind me asking?"

"I stopped at the college," she answered, her eyes glued to the photos on her computer screen. "I'm thinking of switching my major to electronic journalism. So I was close by."

Laura smiled. "That's a wonderful idea, sweetie. I can envision that someday when you and Honey will be operating the newspaper. Two talented sisters heading the family business." She sighed softly. "Just the idea of the Banner Bay future makes me happy."

Happiness is not the emotion that shot to Honey's head when she contemplated working with her sister at the *Bay Banner* in years to come. Her heart stopped for a millisecond. The next jarring thought supposed she and Cricket were already co-owners of the *Bay Banner* or were designated to inherit the paper. Dear Lord.

"Momma, the *Banner* is barely breaking even." *It can't last.*

"We've been through hard times before, Honey."

"The paper needs to move forward; we can't remain stuck in the seventies forever."

"Don't worry. Circulation has picked up as it always does when the tourists return to Crooked Island in the summer."

Depending on the residents of Crooked Island for revenue was a mistake in Honey's opinion. Most only stayed for three months out of the year. She glanced up at the map on the wall nearest her. Crooked Island was a barrier island just off Blue Oyster Bay. A four-mile bridge spanned the sparkling blue waters from the struggling fishing town to the tourist rich island but the divide between the populations was way wider. A few wealthy residents populated the island year-round and a great many summer tourists lived in the gated communities during the summer.

"Would you at least consider increasing the price of the paper, Momma?"

Her mother shook her head. The salt and pepper

curls gathered at the top of her head bounced with determination. "Our regulars can barely afford the dollar twice a week as it is."

"Chef Andy's death is the most newsworthy story to happen here since the Gulf oil spill of 2010."

"Solid information doesn't always require a headline," Laura countered.

"Have you considered publishing only once a week?"

"No, Honey. We've too much local information. And there are always late breaking stories, like Chef Andy's death."

"Unless he's been murdered, there's not much of a story."

"We give people news. Information, really. And I'm proud of the way we do it. We inform them the old-fashioned way. Who, when, where, why, and how. We don't promote our own paper, like the networks do when they push some new sitcom as a news story. We don't give our opinions unless clearly stated on the op-ed page. When you work for the Banner, people know you're an honest journalist. I'm proud of our newspaper. It's been in the family for years, and that's the way I intend for it to stay. In the family, for the good of Blue Oyster Bay."

"Momma. I'm sorry." She hadn't meant to insult her mother. In truth, Honey had felt a bit slimy especially when writing for *The Spin*. A time or two, she'd been called upon—ordered—to stretch the truth, to speculate and to suggest. *The Spin's* reputation had been built more on conjecture than on facts.

Now, without a doubt, after this conversation with her mother, Honey knew freelance writing was her future. With enough contracts, she could see herself living in major cities once more, like New York or Miami. Cricket could run the Banner, she rationalized. Honey might even find love again with an intelligent, handsome risk-taker. A man who looked like a movie star and could not wait to take the next adventure with her.

Anything could happen once she nailed Chef Andy's story.

Shaking off her distracting thoughts, she turned her attention to the computer keyboard, punching quickly through the mullet toss photos. She scanned the usual family photos, fish photos, girls sunning in bikini photos, before coming to an abrupt halt. A full, close-up photo of Eli and Krystal burst onto the screen. Honey's heart jumped.

Krystal photographed like a cover model with striking high cheekbones and glorious blond curls that spilled over her bare shoulders. An adoring Eli looked down on her, oblivious to the camera. His mouth hitched up in a delicious half-smile. Behind his sunglasses, Honey could readily imagine his gaze devouring his new girlfriend. He'd once looked at Honey that way, with eyes only for her. For a minute she couldn't catch her breath. Her shoulders slumped, leaden as if an elephant perched there.

"Honey, which pictures are you going to use?" Cricket asked.

"I don't know." She stretched a finger to close the file. Krystal still smiled up at her. "I'll write the story and then decide," she told Cricket. And then, after one last look at the man she had loved, who had once loved her, Honey hit the delete button. Wasn't using that one. The Mullet Toss story would contain several photos, but none of the sheriff and his date.

****

The ME's office was hot, close, and smelled of strong disinfectant. Eli couldn't wait to leave. "So Sam, you're sure this is an accidental drowning?" he asked.

"Yup. It happens every few months or so." The ME rubbed his deep-set brown eyes. "This poor guy drank too much, fell into the bay, and hit his head on a piling on the way into the water."

"Shame. A waste. Seem like more drinking going on in Blue Oyster Bay lately."

Sam shrugged. "Hardly any jobs around right now. What else is there to do?"

"Guess we need to drum up some businesses that will attract more tourists."

Sam's head of blond curls bounced as he nodded, picking up on Eli's idea. "More tourists, more jobs. Simple math."

"Not going to have tourists if I don't solve Chef Andy's murder soon."

"You will." Sam leaned back in his chair, tapped his lip with the edge of his pen. "Eli, why don't you run for mayor and make the tourist business happen?"

"Are you kidding me? Let Don Turner have the job. Hell, don't I have enough on my plate?" He shook his head. "Man!"

"You mean like murder? Who do you think killed Andy?"

"We're dealing with an amateur," Eli muttered. "We don't have any hardened criminals in the Bay. Everyone is an amateur, so that leaves me with a bunch of suspects."

"Honey Mayhew will help you find the killer. She's

been looking for a good story since high school."

Eli groaned. "Gotta go. You find anything else, give me a call, Sam."

Before Sam could rope him into a conversation about Honey, Eli rushed out of the ME's office, out of the building, and into his car.

Honey Mayhew.

The whole town had been talking about Honey's return from her first day back. He knew it, knew it would happen. Despite her craziness, everyone loved Honey. Couldn't be helped. She'd just been always…well, loveable.

Eli had been in love with her since the first grade. When things had been bad at home for him, she'd coaxed him to see the good in the simple gifts: the sun, the bay, the hardware store's free bubble gum machine.

When his mother left, running off with an artist who'd spent the winter in the Bay, his father took to drinking. Soon Eli became the subject of the gossips. He hated the pity. "That poor Gibson boy." Struggling with his pride became a daily battle. As soon as possible, he gave them something else to talk about. He pitched his way into a full college baseball scholarship.

Only one person celebrated with him. Honey was always by his side. Playing with him, working with him. Every throw he made she caught in practice sessions that lasted from after school to dark. She cheered from the bleachers in every high school and college game. Honey had been the love of Eli's life.

He'd dreamed of giving her the world someday. But someday never came.

She'd broken his heart, choosing to chase a journalism career. Honey's happiness was all he'd ever wanted, so Eli gave her up without a fight.

At first when he returned to the Bay to take care of his sick father, he thought he saw Honey on every street, in all their special places. He'd see her on the beach where they used to swim, the spot where they liked to fish, the Apalachicola National Park, where once full of bravado they watched for black bears, explored overgrown paths, and sometimes got lost on purpose. She was everywhere and nowhere.

Despite the ghost of Honey seeming to haunt him, he stayed in Blue Oyster Bay. He ran for sheriff and was elected. It was just a matter of time before he forgot her.

And then, without warning Honey was back. His heart jumped out of his chest when he first saw her walk into the Blue Oyster Grill. Even wearing a beat-up, old floppy straw hat, and a skeptical expression, she looked every inch the professional reporter. He couldn't look away fast enough. Yeah, he'd heard she was in town, but he assumed it was for a quick visit to her family. He'd been wrong. It was as if no time had passed. She was there. Beside him, standing so close he could smell the lemon citrus scent of her. Representing the *Blue Oyster Bay Banner*, she'd come to cover Chef Andy's sudden demise.

To his surprise Honey's physical appearance hadn't changed. She didn't have the look of hard and cold ambition as he'd expected. This sweet-looking southern beauty had been his. He'd tasted her peachy lips, lingered in the light of her bright spring eyes, brushed her silky sun-bleached hair from her eyes. Warmed by memories, heat like he'd never known spread through him until he broke out in a sweat. She was nervous, he was worse. He'd avoided her eyes, spoke curtly. Denied the rush of desire.

Eli had a job to do.

He had another life now, another woman. He'd moved on.

Although he did his best to avoid being alone with Honey, every time he saw her, Eli wanted her again. Against all reason.

When would his heart be safe? When would she leave? The answer was simple to Eli. Honey would be on her way when he arrested the killer, and she had her big story. Trouble was, Eli had no leads except for the obvious, the cliché of the spouse. But Thea? His instincts were usually good, and every fiber told him no. He just couldn't wrap his head around Andy's wife as a killer.

Honey was hot on his heels. For his own good, he'd better work fast. The sooner she left the Bay, the sooner he could breathe nice and normal again.

Eli vowed to step up his investigation.

Chapter 8

Slightly disturbed by the suggestion Honey might inherit the *Banner Bay* along with her sister, complicated by the medical examiner's memories of their old school days, and in particular her relationship with Eli, Honey left the newspaper office in somewhat of a snit. It hadn't helped her mood to see the pictures of Eli and his main squeeze Krystal looking gorgeous at the Mullet Toss. The Mullet Toss, for heaven's sake! No one is supposed to look glamorous at the Mullet Toss!

Grumbling to herself, Honey climbed on her scooter. She revved the engine as if her ride were a big bad motorcycle. She drove to the outskirts of the Bay's historic district with one objective: Taking her mind off Eli and putting it back on the case where it belonged.

The Oyster Arms, a shabby old apartment complex near the highway held twenty-four apartments, two cinder-block buildings of two stories each. Rachel and Carol, two of the players in the Chef Andy drama rented there. She hoped to run into either of them, but both would be better "accidentally." At the very least, she meant to discover the exact locations of the women's apartments. Honey found Rachel's apartment in the second building and was looking for Carol's in the first, when she heard a door slam. Dressed for business, Rachel stood with her back to the parking lot, locking her apartment door.

Honey changed direction. "Hey, Rachel."

Descending the stairs to the first floor, Rachel ignored her.

Rushing to the mistress's side, Honey matched each long stride the woman took and adopted a chatty tone. "I guess you live here, right?"

No reply.

"I'm looking for Carol. Carol Kahn. Do you know which apartment is hers?"

"No."

"Are you going to the restaurant now?"

Rachel's sudden stop kicked up sand and dust in the gravely space. "Why are you here?"

"Doing a little research for the paper," Honey choked.

"Then do it somewhere else and leave me alone. If you need to bother someone, go down to the docks and bother Ace Barone," she turned on her heel and marched toward town.

"Who is Ace Barone?"

"You're the investigative reporter. Find out!"

"Okay, I will," Honey murmured. That encounter hadn't gone well. But she'd gained another lead. Ace Barone had been mentioned as a possible suspect twice now, which warranted a closer look into the man.

After finding Carol's apartment and making a mental note of its location, she hopped on her scooter and in a matter of minutes was strolling along the docks like a curious tourist. She chatted with the shrimpers, fishermen, and what was left of the men and women who tongued for the almost rare now oysters. No one had seen Ace, but they had a lot to say about their catches. The oysters were small and not nearly enough. Fortunately, the shrimp showed no signs of mutation. However, nothing had been the same since the oil spill. The men wanted to know why no one talked about the oil any longer. Their livelihoods were at stake, but the newspaper and television reporters had lost interest. Sharing the water from the Apalachicola River with Alabama had become the headline story.

Honey assured the men she talked with that the oil spill remained a big story to her. She meant it. She saw the worry in their eyes, the misery in their rough, calloused hands. Her belly clenched tight as she listened. They were right. The story was not over, but there was no Pulitzer to be gained from reporting the ongoing aftermath, years after the fact. She would write the story as soon as she finished wrapping up Chef Andy's murder.

Although her mother bylined and headlined the river stories, Honey felt certain she'd be allowed to write a feature story on the water dilemma at some point.

Unable to answer the men's questions satisfactorily, Honey left the docks determined to find Ace. She walked Main Street beneath a broiling sun and checked every store and restaurant without success. The next step was to track him down at his trailer in East Point. Exhausted, and dripping with sweat, she called her mother and editor-in-chief. "Momma, is there anything you need me to do? If not, I'm going home to work."

"Go on home. We're okay here."

"See you in the morning."

"Wouldn't you like to have dinner with us tonight? We're having slow-cooked barbeque chicken."

"That sound great, but I'll take a rain check."

****

Honey's work at home began on her computer and research of Ace Barone. Turned out he had a record as a young man in New Orleans that included breaking and entering, and graffiti. She couldn't find anything in the past three years until a restraining order taken out last year by a woman he'd been dating showed up, followed by a subsequent arrest for a bar brawl. Alfred Ace Barone was thirty-five years old, had an employment background as a short order cook. A profile emerged of a quick tempered, not too bright individual. But a man capable of murder? She wasn't feeling it.

Shifting her focus, Honey researched poison, well recognized as a woman's weapon of choice. But she would not rule out a man. Arsenic used in Chef Andy's case was simply a white powder that could have easily been mistaken for flour, or sugar, baking soda, or any number of ingredients found in a restaurant kitchen. In Andy's case the dose had been high enough that the ME almost missed the trace in his digestive track. If arsenic had been fed to him over a long period of time, there would have been elements just about everywhere, in his hair and fingernails. But that hadn't been the case, according to Sam. Whoever wanted Andy dead, wanted him gone quickly.

Her mind tumbling with questions and speculation, Honey decided to push away from the computer and give her body a break. Relaxing had never come easily, but she'd always enjoyed a swim. Back in high school her nickname had been Mermaid Mayhew. Corny, but still the memory caused a smile to stretch across her lips.

The beach was deserted at dusk. A wide orange ribbon stretched across the horizon as the sun sank lower. The dark bat-like stingrays would be swimming along the shoreline to feed, but they'd make room for her. Digging into an open box, she pulled out the first swimsuit she came across and changed. Promising herself that she'd unpack the box later, she called to her dog. "Come on, Fred. Let's go for a swim."

Fred refused to go near the water. He plunked down on the sand several feet away and went to sleep. Unlike Honey, he could sleep anywhere anytime. Two minutes after he closed his eyes, the snoring began.

Due to the runoff from the river the bay water appeared slightly iron-brown in color, but clear. Clear enough to see the sting rays gliding close to shore, scattering as Honey waded into the warm, bath water temperature. But once she reached thigh deep water, she started to swim. Keeping her eyes on the horizon she reached for each stroke, pulling hard and deep, using her strength, feeling the muscles pull throughout her body. She'd always loved to swim. How had she let herself forget? For the first time since coming back to her hometown, she felt invigorated as she turned back toward the shore. A lightness of being, the confidence of knowing that at least in this sport, in this one thing, she excelled, and had since high school.

But there was no need to race now. Honey slowed to savor the first real exercise she'd had in months. Promptly hit by a wave, she swallowed a mouthful of saltwater. Choking, she tread water until she recovered her breath. Then, as a welcome sense of peace washed through her, she lay on her back, spread her arms out, and floated. Lost in her private water world, every care drifted out to sea. No real job…no worries, one would come. No firm suspect in Chef Andy's murder, no worries. Killers always made mistakes. The guilty party would soon surface. No love…no worries, a great once-in-a-lifetime-love would soon come along.

Replenished, Honey headed to shore exerting fresh energy into a powerful backstroke.

"Honey Marie!"

Only two people ever called her by her full name and that was her mother when she was angry with her. And Eli.

The sheriff.

She turned to the sound of his voice and tread water. Eli stood on the shore waving at her. "Come on in!"

She hated being ordered to do anything, but in this case, she had no choice. Why had he come here to her sanctuary, her home? Nervousness bubbled in her belly. Inner peace evaporated.

Eli, in full sheriff's uniform, waited for her, hands on hips. This might be an official visit. But why? What kind of trouble could she possibly be in? Could she fake drowning? No, she was trapped. She had to face whatever music Eli was playing. Taking long, languid strokes, Honey swam toward the shore. When the water became too shallow to swim. she stood.

Honey moved slowly toward him, splashing her feet a bit more than necessary.

Fred had found the energy to sit up on his haunches beside the sheriff, and stare at Eli as if he were waiting for a treat. But Eli didn't see Fred. His gaze never wavered from Honey. His unblinking eyes took on the color of the dark ocean.

The heat of his gaze shot through her. Intense and searing. She warmed in places that hadn't been warmed in months. The notion he could still melt her bones disturbed her. Angered her. He had moved on; he had no right to scrutinize her near naked body like a judge in a beauty pageant. He had no right to stop by on a whim.

When she'd put on the scarlet bikini, she hadn't expected company. While she didn't possess the curves of Krystal, she knew she filled out the bikini well.

Eli bent down and picked up her towel from the sand and handed it to her.

"What brings you to my neck of the beach, Sheriff?"

"You. You don't listen well. Never did, I suppose. I've told you to back off. It's my job to discover who killed Andy and I will. Without your help. If you don't stop meddling, you're going to make things more difficult for me."

"I don't want to make things more difficult for you." She wrapped the towel around her. "I'm just doing my job. My editor—"

"Your mother."

She shot him a withering glare. "She expects me to report promptly on what happened and why it happened to our readers."

"And I'll give you that information when I have it. In the meantime, don't get yourself killed."

"Killed?"

Eli's eyes narrowed as he gazed at her. "That's what happens to busybodies in a murder investigation."

"Do you know something I should know?"

He scrubbed a hand through his hair. "I've had a complaint about you."

"Me? Who complained?"

"An individual who may be a person of interest called this afternoon to complain that you were harassing her."

"Rachel."

"Yes. Rachel. But I'm not at liberty to say. Do you understand?"

"I never heard about Rachel from you." Honey paused for a breath. "But do you think she did it?"

"I have no evidence."

"But she had a motive. Andy had just dumped her."

His gaze fastened on hers. "People dump each other all the time. They don't kill for being dumped."

"Like you dumped me?"

"I believe it was you who dumped me."

"What?" An unexpected chill skipped down her spine.

"This isn't the time or place to get personal. But let's just get this out of the way now."

On a deserted beach in the deepening darkness.

"I know a thing or two about being dumped," Eli growled. "Only because you refused to wait for my decision."

"Can you truly blame me? One day you're going back to the team, the next day you're not. I needed to take the job I was offered or lose it. The best offer I'd ever received. I waited for you to make up your mind as long as I could. You can't procrastinate forever. Do you procrastinate as sheriff? Are you holding up this investigation, Eli?"

His eyes narrowed on her. His voice was clipped. "At the time my future was on the line. Our future together was on the line. I think things through, while you jump off cliffs. You're still doing it. You're always in a hurry, a rush for the next big thing. Impulsive as all get out. Someday you've got to learn how to reign it in."

"And someday you'll have to learn to make a decision in under thirty days," she snipped. Shaking with rage, she turned on her heel and strode down the packed sand beach toward the house. How could Eli say such a thing? It was so unjust. And he represented justice. Ha! "Come on, Fred!"

The dog hauled himself up and lumbered behind Honey.

Eli caught up to her. "I didn't come here to argue."

Honey picked up speed. "Well, why not, if that's what it takes to clear the air between us."

Eli kept up. "What's the point? After all this time, what's the point?"

Honey came to an abrupt halt, faced him, drew in a deep breath, and fixed her gaze on his. "Maybe, just maybe we could be friends."

He broke eye contact. "That ship has sailed."

"No. No, I don't believe that. We're adults now. Let's adult. Just try and understand, Eli. If I hadn't accepted that job when I did, I would have wound up back here. The last thing in the world I could do…deal with."

One corner of his mouth hitched up. "And yet here you are."

"Temporarily." She tossed her wet hair and started walking again. "I'm working hard and fast on leaving."

"Really? Working hard and fast on leaving? A minute ago, it looked like you were working on your backstroke. I had the impression you were enjoying yourself out there in the water. Like old times Mermaid Mayhew."

The fact he'd found Honey enjoying herself irritated her for some reason. "Have you said what you came to say?"

He nodded his head. "Yeah, but did you hear me?"

"No harassing Rachel."

"Anyone. Don't harass anyone," he repeated.

"Even you?"

"I don't think I can stop you."

She closed her eyes, swept up in his familiar scent of woodsy, all male, remembering the feeling of being wrapped in his arms, enveloped in warmth and steel. She waited to be taken back to that time when he would have opened his arms and scooped her into her happy place.

She opened her eyes. His gaze lingered on her lips. He stood close enough to touch, to kiss, to …

Speak. "You have company," he said at the sound of car tires crunching on the oyster shell drive.

"I'm not expecting anyone."

The dog waddled away toward the driveway.

When she caught sight of the car, sweet relief spread through Honey. "It's Miss Bess." "Remember what I said," Eli warned.

She stopped, looked up at him. "Do we have a deal then? You'll keep me in the loop?"

"And you won't harass anyone." He flipped his reply over his shoulder.

"Of course not. We'll be friends?"

"We'll see," he said.

Before she could say more, Eli was greeting Honey's grandmother. "Good evenin', Miss Bess. How are you this fine evening?"

Miss Bess gave him a coy smile and batted her lashes. "A lot better after seeing you with mah Honey."

"Take care of yourself, Miss Bess." Giving her a quick buss on the cheek, Eli strode away.

Honey welcomed her grandmother with a hug while glancing over Bess's shoulder to watch Eli leave.

Leaving her feeling unsettled and confused. A knot rested in the pit of her stomach. She sagged beneath the weight of disappointment as he got in his car and drove away.

Miss Bess *tsked*. Actually *tsked*. "Eli is such a nice young man. I've always said that." Without pausing for breath, she continued. "What was he doing here?"

Honey deflected. "You've got to stop flirting with Eli, Miss Bess."

"Why?"

"It's unbecoming for a woman your age." Although her grandmother flirted with all the men in Blue Oyster Bay.

"My age? Sugah, ah'm not dead."

"No. And I'm happy to see you but what brings you to my little beach house? Confidential Informant news?"

"No, but ah brought you some of my famous chocolate cake."

"Well, that's the best reason in the world. Come on up to the house and we'll feast."

"Ah like it that Eli's coming to courtin' you again."

"He's not courting me. He'll never come courting me again."

"Did you give that good-lookin' man some sort of ultimatum?"

"Years ago. I had to move on. Besides, I knew he'd come after me." The nervous laughter in her throat released as a gurgle. "But he didn't. When the team dropped him, he joined the Navy. Eli went to war rather than marry me."

"Fool thing to do. Fool thing to let that man go. No southern lady in her right mind gives a man an ultimatum. 'Sides, if you put your mind to it, ah'm thinkin' Eli would be onto you again like syrup on hotcakes."

Despite all of the water under the bridge between Eli and her, Honey warmed to her grandmother's scenario. But only for a minute. Seconds ago, he so unjustly accused her of driving them apart. "I don't think so."

"You'll see, if you're patient. Your eggs are dryin' up as we speak. Don't be forgettin' you're a Mayhew. And don't be forgettin' the dance next week to raise funds for the senior center. You get a dress, make it short and tight and start workin' it, girl."

Chuckling, Honey squeezed the old woman's hand. "I love you, Grandma."

"Miss Bess."

It must have been the sugar in the chocolate cake that kept Honey up and pacing long after her grandmother had left. With nothing to do but stew and think about Eli, she decided to open a few boxes and put her treasures away. What if the sheriff didn't uphold his part of the bargain and keep her in the loop? If he caught her snooping, would he lock her up? He might just enjoy locking Honey in the local slammer.

Sighing, strongly enough to shake her shoulders, she tossed off the disturbing thoughts and opened a box. There on the top, fairly squashed, sat the baseball cap Eli had given her six years ago, just before the team dropped him. Just after his injury healed, but not to team satisfaction.

Slapping the cap on her head, she went to bed and thought again about what her grandmother had said. Was it possible she could win Eli's heart again? Did she want to win his love? No! She was not staying in Blue Oyster Bay and Eli would never leave.

Hours later, she fell into a troubling sleep. Woken by the nonstop ringing of her cell phone, Honey groggily braced herself on her arm as she fumbled for the phone. Instead, she found Eli's baseball cap on the bed beside her in the empty space. The whimper Honey heard came from her, followed by a sigh. Fully awake, she found the phone. Marylu's name flashed on caller ID. Honey made no attempt to hide her sleep voice. If she spoke as little as possible, she might be able to go back to sleep after the call. "Hey, girlfriend," she mumbled.

"Yeah. Sorry to wake you, Honey, but I thought you'd want to know."

"What? What time is it?"

"It must have happened last night. They found his body on the beach this morning."

"Whose body?" Body is all she needed to hear. Quickly awake, Honey went into high alert mode, from zero to one hundred percent in a millisecond.

"It wasn't like he'd been swimming. He was still dressed in his seersucker suit."

Only one person in Oyster Bay wore a seersucker suit. Honey swung her legs over the bedside and jumped to her feet. "Donald Turner? Don Turner's dead?"

Chapter 9

Honey arrived at the hospital, a.k.a. the medical examiner and coroner's offices, in record time. Hurrying to the wing housing the medical examiner's office, Honey texted her mother, a.k.a. *Banner Bay* editor. Head down punching in her message, she collided with a steel wall. Oh. No. The wall was Eli.

"Imagine my surprise," Eli drawled. His gaze settled on her, dark and forbidding.

If a stormy glare could send a girl packing, she would be best served by buying a one-way ticket to Tangiers. Immediately. There could be no mistaking the message he sent. Nor the message delivered when her body slammed against his. Hot and hard.

Evidently, the sheriff hadn't experienced the same jolt.

He glowered.

She blushed.

Squirming beneath his obvious ire, Honey forced what she hoped to be an innocent smile. "Good morning, Eli."

"Uh huh." He acknowledged her with a deep, guttural, grunt. "Here to harass me?"

The lump in her throat threatened to cut off air, the heavily disinfectant scented air. Freshly polished, the floor of the hospital corridor gleamed. The blinding white floor walls and ceiling gave off an ethereal feeling.

She struggled to get it together. While she'd realized she might run into the sheriff, Honey figured he'd be long gone by the time she arrived. She hadn't planned for another Eli encounter. Allowing this tall, magnificent man she'd once loved to intimidate her just because he wore a uniform was crazy.

Straightening her shoulders and lifting her chin, Honey gazed directly into Eli's angry eyes. "I'm here to take my friend MaryLu to breakfast. Her shift is ending."

"Uh-huh. Let me guess, MaryLu would be your source."

He made it a statement, but Honey regarded it as a question which she avoided by asking one of her own. "May I ask what you're doing at the hospital so early, Sheriff?"

"Did MaryLu call you? Did she tell you I was here?"

Best defense, answer a question with a question. "Why would she do that?"

"Because they fished Don Turner's body out of the bay this morning. Your nurse friend saw them bring him in to the medical examiner's office."

Honey feigned a surprised gasp, hoping the anger would ebb from Eli's eyes. "No! I didn't know!"

"He's dead. Turner's dead," Eli announced with unexpected harshness. The hard set of his jaw telegraphed his frustration. Honey had experienced his way of expressing disappointment in the past. A bad pitch, a losing game. This was way worse.

But this was another life lost in a matter of days. And no time for games. A cold sweep of sadness shot through her for the victim and for Eli who had vowed to serve and protect. He could not have foreseen a threat to Turner.

Although Honey had never been fond of the attorney, he didn't deserve to die. As far as she knew, he was not accident prone. Turner took very good care of himself. "What happened?" she asked, continuing her act of surprise, unwilling to cause trouble for MaryLu.

"He drowned." Eli spoke through his teeth, barely moving his lips.

"Wearing his seersucker suit? He went swimming in his suit?"

"Did I say what he was wearing?"

"No, I just made a lucky guess. No one has ever seen Donald Turner wearing anything but a seersucker suit."

"Lucky guess," he repeated under his breath. "For your information, I'm thinking he might have been drinking, took a walk on the dock and fell in."

Honey shook her head. "I can't believe it. I can't believe he didn't know how to swim, drunk or not. And I don't believe you buy that scenario either. No one can live in the Bay most of their life surrounded by water and not know how to swim."

"I'll give you that," he said, and added with a cynical twist of his lips, "It's hard to believe, all right. Just like it's hard for me to believe you're here to take Marylu to breakfast this morning of all mornings. 'Specially since she rarely works this shift."

"Exactly. And when she does, we have breakfast together." She reached out, lightly touching him on the forearm. "Who found Donald? Where did they find him?"

Eli jerked back his arm as if he'd received an electric shock. Planting his fists on his hips, he angled his head. The anger had ebbed from his eyes, but they flashed with sharp annoyance as he rested his gaze on her. "You know, you sound a lot like one of those vulture reporters. Not like Blue Oyster Bay's own Honey Mayhew."

He'd changed tactics. And how could she deny it? She had become a vulture reporter. Currently, the only one on the scene. And while she didn't want to make trouble for MaryLu, she couldn't deny her presence... and profession. "Don't you think that the people of our town have a right to know if there's a murderer stalking our streets?"

"Stalking our streets? That's a pretty melodramatic statement even for you." He shook his head as if there were no hope for her. "A shrimper found him floating by the dock."

She lowered her eyes, her voice. "Eli, was he...do you suspect foul play?"

"The M.E. is working on him now. I have no suspicions. I'm waiting for the facts."

"Why would anyone want to kill Donald Turner?"

Eli arched a brow. "Did I mention the words murder or kill?"

Honey shook her head. "No, it's just so strange that he drowns just days after Chef Andy is killed. A man running for mayor just doesn't throw himself in the bay."

"There are all kinds of innocent explanations. As I said, Turner simply might have had too much to drink at the Ale House and got a little too close to the bay on his way home."

"Donald was Andy's partner in the restaurant, you know."

He nodded slowly. "I do know that, Brenda Starr."

Brenda Starr was an old newspaper cartoon character, an intrepid reporter with an hourglass figure and flaming red hair who solved mysteries daily. Honey did not resemble Brenda Starr in any way. "You don't need to mock me."

"I'm just sayin'. Don Turner wasn't the Bay's only mayoral candidate. If you're looking for murder and a motive, maybe some folks didn't want to see him elected as mayor."

"Lynnell Jones?" Honey asked, incredulous. "Are you suggesting Lynnell Jones?"

Eli shrugged again.

"She always runs for mayor. No one pays any attention to her. Are you really suggesting Lynell might have pushed him in the bay to eliminate the competition?"

He raised his arms, palms up.

"You're playing with me. This is serious stuff and you're kidding, right?"

"No, I'm not kidding. Since I've been the sheriff, nothing surprises me anymore."

"Everyone knows Lynnell is a little nutty. She's always been strange and always looking like a ghost with her white hat, white dress, white stockings, and shoes. Remember when we were in school, she chased us all out of the Slushy Shack every chance she got? She didn't even work there."

Eli gave an inch of a grin. "Lynnell Jones has run for mayor in every election since the turn of the century. She has never won. There isn't a soul in Blue Oyster Bay who would vote for crazy old Lynnell. You're right, not a man woman or child would suspect for a millisecond that she would shove her opponent in the bay."

"Of course not," she agreed as if she hadn't been taken in by Eli's suggestion. "Well, I hope you're able to get to the bottom of Turner's demise soon," she said with a hint of huffiness.

"There is no bottom, Miss Mayhew. Don't mess with this. As of now Don Turner's death is classified as an accidental drowning."

"And that's exactly what I'll report in my story."

"Obituary," he corrected her.

"Exactly. Obit and story."

"There is no story." Eli tipped a hand to his hat in a feeble salute. "See ya." Stepping around Honey as if she might be contagious, he started down the corridor toward the double doors.

"But if you discover anything…anything important," she called after him. "You'll call me, right?"

He stopped dead in his tracks and turned. His voice echoed deep, low and cold. "Now you're eager and ready to take my calls?"

She nodded slowly, feeling her blood run cold. Her body stiffened against an onslaught of unwanted memories. There'd been a time when she'd ignored Eli's calls, a time when she had to move on or crumble. The past kept rearing its ugly head in reminders she'd rather not have. Eli remembered what Honey chose to forget. Okay, so it hadn't been her finest hour. She'd hurt him, blown him off. Because she'd felt betrayed.

Instead of making plans for them to be together no matter what, Eli stalled. Wishy-washy, he couldn't seem to make a decision for the life of him. Honey had never lacked decisiveness. After waiting for what she believed a long enough time, she came to a conclusion and made a decision. He didn't love her. She'd moved forward. Alone.

With a rueful smile and a snap of his head, Eli turned and strode out of the hospital without a backward glance.

When Mary Lou's shift ended, Honey took her to the only place in town open at seven o'clock in the morning. It had been years since she'd enjoyed a breakfast of a steaming mug of coffee and heaping plate of biscuits and gravy, fried eggs, and four strips of bacon. In her city life, Honey always chose a container of yogurt on the go or nothing but large quantities of designer coffee for breakfast.

"Having breakfast with you is getting to be a regular thing. I like it," Marylu said as she dug into the same huge breakfast plate. "Did you see Eli?"

"Ran into him in the lobby as he was leaving."

"What did he say?"

"Not much."

"Honey, it scares me to think there's a killer on the loose. We've always been so safe here."

"Eli doesn't seem worried. He called me Brenda Starr and avoided my questions."

Marylu smiled. "Brenda Starr? Wow. Well, he'll come around."

"I don't think so." Honey shook her head. "He avoided me when I came back to Blue Oyster Bay, and now he's making it difficult for me to do my job."

"He was crazy in love with you."

"Back in the day. Back then we had plans. But when his pro team released him, he joined the Navy and became a ghost. He didn't bother to call me until he was being deployed."

"Has he ever explained?"

"I didn't take the calls. I hadn't taken his calls when I thought he was just procrastinating on making a life together or not. I assumed he was calling with more of the same vacillation. I was angry. Rightfully so."

"Even so, didn't you want to hear what he had to say?"

"It wouldn't have made any difference. By then I'd made new plans. I'd just settled in Boston and was about to start a new job."

Marylu clucked like a sage old woman. "You both were hurt. Maybe you're both still hurting?"

"Our story ended a long time ago."

"Six years? Seven?"

"Six." Not that she ever counted.

MaryLu leaned back in the booth and crossed her arms. "Some stories never end."

"You are a hopeless romantic."

"No, But I've never seen Eli indecisive since he returned. Maybe it's the job, but I don't know the man you're describing. He's changed, Honey. There may be hope for you two yet."

Honey shook her head. "Don't go there."

"Okay. I won't say another word. Except that the night shift is not my favorite shift. Gotta get home and to bed."

"And I've got to get into the office and write a story about Don. Sad. And strange."

"You're welcome. It's been too long since biscuits and gravy graced my plate."

"Are you going to the Lighthouse fundraiser tonight?"

"I sure don't feel like dancing, but if I don't go, Miss Bess will have my hide."

Warm and fully fed, Honey felt tempted to go back home and back to bed like Marylu. Her early morning encounter with Eli, unkind old memories, and her old friend's insistence that all was not over between her and the sheriff, left Honey with a deep down, truly disturbing roiling in the pit of her stomach.

She climbed on her little red scooter, and struggling to stay focused on the writing ahead, she made her way to the office. What was wrong with her? From head to toe she simmered with restless energy, like a volcano preparing to erupt. The fried eggs, perhaps?

She parked behind the building, locked her scooter and was searching for the keys in her backpack when Miss Bess strolled out of the back door.

"Mornin', Sugah."

"Good morning, Grand." Honey bestowed a warm hug on her diminutive grandmother. She always was happy to see the woman who had been the steadying figure throughout her life. "Miss Bess, did you hear about Donald Turner?"

"Ah did. Ah did. You know girl, news travels faster than the wind. Bless his heart."

"Have you written his obituary for the column?"

"Oh, land's sake, no! Not yet. Ah'm fixin' to have my hair and nails done at the Curly Q."

"Again?"

"I need to look my best for the Senior Center Fundraiser tonight. I'm playin' at the Lighthouse."

"The fundraiser won't be cancelled because of, of Turner's death?"

"Land's sake, no. He wouldn't have wanted us to cancel." Bess lowered her voice to a whisper, "Not meaning any disrespect, ah would dislike speakin' ill of the dead, but although old Don might have been running for mayor, he was hardly the Bay's favorite son."

"I, I understand. Don't worry Grand, I'll write the obit for you."

"Thank you, Sugah. Ah could use your help today, and I'm sure Mr. Turner would appreciate a real professional writing his obituary."

"Have you heard anything about a funeral?"

"Dolly at the funeral home said he'd left orders for his remains to be shipped back to his sister in Ohio. Don't think he expected to leave this world so soon, though."

"No."

"A young man, he was only sixty-five."

"Sixty-five years young," Honey said, gently patting her grandmother on the back. She loved Miss Bess and counted on the old woman living for a very long time. "Age is all in your perspective."

"You're right about that," she agreed emphatically. "You're gonna be at the fundraiser tonight?"

"I would not miss it for the world."

"Wear something sexy."

"Sexy?"

"You know, short, tight, and low-cut. Like ah been tellin' you. The Mayhew women have a reputation to uphold."

Not this Mayhew. "Yes, Miss Bess." Finding a dress would mean opening another box to search for something appropriate. So far in the last six weeks since she'd been home, there'd been no need for her to wear a dress. Her grandmother wore an apprehensive expression. To ease her mind, Honey gave a thumbs-up sign, although she knew good and well finding a dress that was short, tight, and low-cut wasn't going to happen. Sexy dresses had never found a place in her wardrobe.

"All right, then. Ah'll see you tonight."

"Can't wait." But she could. Oh, how she could.

Her steps slowed as she entered the building, passed through the small lounge where coffee perked and a box of donuts sat opened, minus a few. Only the grease spots remained in the box. If it were any other morning, she would have grabbed two. This morning she walked straight into the newsroom. A coffee mug and a chocolate covered donut sat on her mother's desk, but the editor-in-chief had just opened the main door, signaling the official start of the business day.

She greeted Honey with a warm smile. "Good morning, Honey. You're in early."

"I had breakfast with Marylu."

"Such a nice young woman. You two have been friends since high school and that's a very good thing. It's difficult to find long-term friends."

"It's good to have a girlfriend again," Honey acknowledged.

Her mother raised an inquiring—and professionally waxed—eyebrow. "I expect you know about Don Turner?"

"I do." She sunk into her desk chair. "Something's not right in the Bay, Momma."

"Don't you know it!"

"Do you believe our only true mayoral candidate accidentally slipped and fell into the bay? We're talking about the man who also happened to be Chef Andy's partner, and not a happy partner at that. Andy owed him money."

Her mother slid into her executive chair. "It's all very mysterious and alarming."

"And now with Don gone, I guess Thea doesn't have to pay him what he's owed."

"Oh, good grief, Honey! You are not suggesting that

Thea had anything to do with Donald Turner's death." She paused, frowning. "Or Andy's?"

Honey shrugged. "I'm just saying it's a possibility."

"That's a horrid possibility."

"Just remove your mind from that horrid possibility."

"Who killed Don Turner and why? I can't put the questions out of my mind, Momma, but I'll have to put them on the back burner until we hear from the medical examiner."

"Just write Donald's obituary. Miss Bess is getting as she says, 'beautified' this morning."

"I ran into her as she was leaving. She advised me to wear a sexy dress tonight."

Her mother laughed. "Then you'd better not have any donuts today."

"No, Ma'am." Revealing she'd already had her calorie count for the next week at breakfast would not do. With the exception of morning donuts, her momma was an advocate of healthy eating.

Honey turned on her computer. The old instrument took at least five minutes to crank up. As she did every morning, she used a pencil to jot down her to-do list while the computer rumbled awake. Topping her list was a return to the docks to talk further to Aaron about the lingering problems brought on by the oil spill. Hopefully she'd also find the elusive Ace Barone, former chef at the Blue Oyster Grill. Last on her list was a visit to Cricket's closet. Her young sister only wore sexy dresses and Honey figured she could squeeze into one of them since tightness was a condition to be desired, according to her fashionista grandmother.

After writing Don Turner's obituary without details,

which amounted to a vague two paragraphs, Honey told her mother where she was going in search of stories, slapped on her floppy hat, and set out for the docks on her scooter. Too hot to walk.

****

"We used to provide most of the shrimp and ninety-five percent of the oysters served in Florida and along the Gulf Coast. Can't do that anymore," Aaron, one of the dock fishermen told her at the finish of her interview with him. "It's not right. It just ain't right."

"No, it's not and I hope my article helps make the public aware of what's happened."

"Papers and the TV don't write nothin' about the spill anymore."

"But I will. Thank you." Honey shook hands with Aaron and as she turned, she ran into a wall. A hulking wall of steel disguised as a thick, red-bearded man with a shaved bald dome. "S...sorry," she stammered.

"You Honey Mayhew?"

She answered warily, "Yes."

"Heard you were looking for me. Ace Barone."

"Ace Barone." She couldn't help staring. "Yes." He resembled a swarthy pirate, emphasis on swarthy. His face appeared compressed, his close-set eyes shone like onyx beads. "I've been looking for you because I wanted to ask you a few questions about Chef Andy. I understand you worked at the Blue Oyster Grill for a while."

"Yeah. About six months."

"Were you fired?"

"Yeah. Andy and I didn't always agree on what to serve and what to toss." He pursed thick chapped lips.

"Are you saying he served...dated seafood?"

121

"Yeah. It's done. Look, I disagreed with him on a few things, only natural, but he wouldn't change up the menu. He wouldn't try anything that he hadn't been cooking and serving for twenty years. I argued with him…a lot and one day after we shouted at each other for a while, he fired me."

"How did you feel about that?" Ace Barone smelled of fish.

"Best thing that ever happened to me."

"Really?"

"I did some things as a kid I'm not proud of, but I've turned my life around. I'm straight now. I'm a first-rate chef and I'm about to start work at Beasly's."

"Rachel's restaurant?"

"Right."

"Well, congratulations."

"Gonna be a partner."

"You don't say." A partner with Rachel? Momentarily stunned, Honey's mind whirled with possibilities.

"Yeah. I do. If you came lookin' for me thinking I offed Andy cause he fired me, you're off base. There are more folks in town than me who had real reason to kill him."

"And they are?" she asked, swiftly shaking the interesting partnership information off to continue the interview.

"Lady, I'm not crazy enough to name names."

"Don't you want to see the crime solved, your name cleared, and the killer caught?"

"Doesn't matter none to me. I didn't do it and I can't say I'm sorry he's gone."

"Oh." Honey had no answer to his arrogance.

Neither did she want to be breathing in any more of his fishy smell. "Well, good luck in your new position."

He shot her a smirk and strode down the dock toward Aaron's boat. Ace could chew nails. The man gave off a dangerous vibe in addition to his fishy aroma. She wondered if Eli had interviewed him.

But why should she wonder. Worrying about Eli's investigation was just wrong. One more stop and she'd call her sleuthing done for the day.

Minutes later, Honey knocked on the entrance door to the Grill. Carol opened the door. There were more sparkling rhinestones nesting in her hair than ever before. And still, the dark wiry mass stood out around her head like a thick black cloud. "What do you want?"

"I came to pay my respects to Thea. Wondering if there's anything I can do?"

"What, are you here to take a server shift without pay?" she snapped.

"If there's a way I can help to keep the Grill opened, I'll do it," Honey said more calmly than she felt. Telling Carol where to go would be so much more satisfying. "I'm here for Thea as are most people who live in the Bay."

"Thea doesn't need you, or anyone else in town. She's as good a chef as Andy was. As a matter of fact, he learned a lot from her."

"That…that does not surprise me." But it did.

"And if you're here to find out if we're opening the Grill again. We are. We'll open in two more weeks."

"Good. Good. I'm glad to hear that. Thea must be grateful for your help."

For the first time Carol smiled and her tone became more pleasant than harsh. "I'm Thea's new partner and you can headline that fact. 'Cause it's a fact."

"Con...congratulations."

"And if you want to know who we think killed Andy without asking the grieving widow, I'll tell you. Rachel Grover."

"Really?" While Honey wasn't exactly stunned by Carol's revelation, she considered the information intriguing.

"Rachel got crazy when Andy broke it off. But Thea had had enough. She was ready to leave Andy and this hick town in the dust. You don't know what that man put her through."

"No..."

"No one did. Except me. He worked her round the clock. Never appreciated her."

"Do you think Rachel might have had something to do with—"

"Don Turner's death? Yeah, and don't look so surprised. The whole town's talking about it."

"News does indeed travel fast."

"Heard he drowned. Turner did way too much drinking and the booze finally did him in."

Honey's research had never turned up any hint of the lawyer having a drinking problem. "But he was a partner in this restaurant," she pointed out. "He was owed money, from what I hear."

Almost imperceptibly Carol stiffened. "Right. And Andy's insurance policy would have paid him off. But now...well, Thea and I will do just fine. You just watch."

"I will, and I'm sure you will do just fine." Honey shot her a smile. "But when may I speak with Thea?"

"When she's good and ready. And that's gonna take some time. So don't come 'round no more until you see the grand reopening sign on the door."

"Please tell Thea I stopped by and give her my regards."

"Sure."

A swirl of dejection, boulder-large, circled the pit of Honey's stomach as she left the Grill. She'd gained a new sense of distrust, not to mention a hearty dislike for Carol. And she'd learned something that might prove extremely important. Seemingly, an insurance policy left by Chef Andy would solve any financial problems for Thea. Honey needed to jump onto the money trail.

Carol apparently had taken on the role of the wolf at the door protecting Thea—whether the widow needed protection or not. The women's relationship struck Honey as disturbing and sad. Thea, who could not hurt anyone, had landed under Carol's thumb. To think the shy widow was responsible for poisoning her husband and pushing her inebriated attorney-partner into the bay was outrageous. Who would believe for a minute that behind the mousy woman's shy exterior lurked a malicious killer? No one! And yet, Carol stood guard to protect her. And to take advantage of poor Thea?

No closer to an answer, only contemplating even more questions, Honey made her way back to the paper to transfer her notes from her tablet to her computer.

Her mother was preparing to leave, early for a woman who put in twelve-to-fourteen-hour days to keep the *Bay Banner* alive. When her father passed of lung cancer when Honey was just ten years old, Laura had taken over her husband's position at the newspaper he'd loved. She'd blamed his "big, fat old cigars" for his illness and poured her grief into the *Banner* and volunteering for the cancer society.

Honey had no place to put her grief or no understanding at the time of what a hole Martin Mayhew's death would leave in her life.

"Honey, how long will you be here? I want to close up."

Musings interrupted, Honey answered quickly. "Um, ten minutes. Give me ten, Momma. But I can close up. You go."

"Okay, I'd appreciate that. I want to go home and get ready for the fundraiser."

The Lighthouse Senior Citizen Fundraiser, the event that kept slipping Honey's mind seemed to be the one everyone in town could not forget. The last thing in the world she wanted to do tonight was wiggle into a sexy dress, even if she had any, and socialize. According to Miss Bess, almost everyone in town had bought tickets to be there.

"What time does the action start?"

"Seven. It's an early evening, due to most of the older folks."

"Right." *Great! She could be home and in bed by ten.*

"Don't worry, there'll be plenty of others your age. The buffet is always delicious and of course dancing until you drop. Miss Bess's band is pretty darn good."

"Uh huh."

"Excuse me?"

"Yes, Ma'am," she said quickly, revising her answer to the way she'd been raised.

"Eli will be there, you know. His father is a resident."

"Bill Gibson? He's a resident in the Lighthouse?"

Her mother gave a sad nod of her head.

126

"I didn't know that."

Laura sighed. "Yes, it's sad. Terribly sad. Eli came home to take care of Bill, but after a year or so it became impossible. He was forced to place his dad in residency."

"What happened?"

"Dementia. He'd lived such a hard life, you know. Until Eli got into baseball and had some money. He bought the house on E Street for his dad. You knew that, didn't you?"

"I vaguely remember you telling me something about Bill." She had forgotten until now. Her heart contracted. Eli's dad had been someone she had cared deeply about. Bill Gibson had been the town drunk, but he'd also loved his son and never missed a high school game.

The painful squeeze of her heart jolted Honey. How had her ambition driven all thought and care about the people who had lovingly impacted her growing years?

"Between you and me, Honey, I think all the years of hardship on that shrimp boat before he was able to retire affected him," her mother said. Laura would never discuss or mention his drinking problem.

"I'm sorry. So sorry, Momma. He was such a sweet man."

"I remember thinking you'd be lucky to have him as your father-in-law."

"Yes…" Caught between tears and a closed throat, Honey hunched closer to her computer screen so her mother could not see her guilt—and pain. If it would help Bill Gibson, Honey would write a check for as much as she had in the bank and dance all night at the fundraiser.

"I'm leaving now. See you tonight."

"Yes, Momma."

If she'd known Bill was a resident at the center, she would have paid him a visit by now. She would make up for her ignorance tomorrow. Why hadn't Eli mentioned his father? Most likely because he assumed she didn't care.

Honey had left extra food in Fred's bowl so she could spend an hour at the fund-raising event without worrying about him. Before she left the Banner office, she decided to transfer her interviews and do a final check of her email.

She didn't recognize the address of the first mail. The message appeared to be from one of the anonymous email services. Risking she was not about to download a virus, in which case she would never hear the end of it from her mother, Honey took the chance it could be a tip. The entire town and most of the Gulf Coast knew she was investigating the death of Chef Andy. And now, she assumed, the strange passing of the late mayoral candidate Don Turner. Holding her breath, hoping against hope she wasn't inviting a virus into her poor old computer, Honey hit the button, closed her eyes, and counted to ten before she opened her eyes again. The words leaped from the screen.

THIS IS A WARNING. GET OUT OF BLUE OYSTER BAY. LEAVE NOW WHILE YOU'RE STILL ALIVE.

Chapter10

Stunned, Honey's jaw dropped. Literally. And then the palpitations begin. She took several deep breaths, attempting to restore calm.

Who would want her out of town? Easy answer. And frightening. A killer. A serial killer?

Head spinning, her mind raced through the obvious suspects. Rachel who'd reported Honey for harassment and who'd threatened to take out a restraining order on her? Carol whose eyes burned with fury when Honey had questioned her just hours ago? Ace Barone, official tough guy pirate who just looked scary as a real plunderer? Eli, for sure, would like to see her leave town, but he wouldn't send an anonymous email. He would look her straight in the eye and physically point her in the right direction. He might even escort her out of town with sirens blaring and lights flashing.

The warning gave no clue of the email's origination. Perhaps she should tell Eli about the threat. With two people dead, she couldn't dismiss the message as a bad joke. Maybe she needed the sheriff's protection. Or not. Eli might use the warning to her as an excuse to give Honey another lecture or worse, to order her to leave town until the danger had passed. Honey refused to give him the pleasure of either experience.

No! Honey pulled her runaway thoughts up short. She was allowing her imagination full reign. The email might not have even been meant for her. The internet did strange things. Messages got tangled in clouds and whatnot. People made mistakes in addressing emails. She could think of several reasons not to worry about the warning. But she did anyway. Two people were dead.

Now more than ever, the last thing in the world Honey wanted to do was attend the senior center fundraiser. But she'd do it for Grandma Bess and Eli's dad. Besides, she would be run out of town if she did not put in an appearance. In any event, she had nowhere to run to. The Bay was her town of last resort. The *Banner* her only hope of paying the rent.

If the raccoons didn't get to his bowl first, Fred had plenty to eat. She'd left food and water out for him before leaving home that morning. The old dog never left the porch except to pee, so Honey never worried about him too much. As a matter of fact, she'd grown to like having a companion at home. Her aged, overweight, laid-back bulldog cut through her loneliness. He occasionally barked, which might scare away a stranger—who couldn't catch a glimpse of the aged canine. In another lifetime Fred might have been a legitimate guard dog.

Exchanging her straw hat for a neon green helmet that glowed in the dark, Honey climbed on her scooter and headed for the rambling old Victorian home where she'd grown up, the home her sister, mother, and Miss Bess shared on Beauregard Boulevard.

No matter how she tried, she'd never remove the image of her grandfather rocking on the porch looking so much like the fried chicken colonel. It was frightening. The colonel was old Beauregard Mayhew's doppleganger. Her granddaddy had fought in the Spanish-American War and pretty much worshiped

Teddy Roosevelt until the day he died. Colorful, outspoken, and cantankerous, Honey had loved Beau heart and soul. His arms were always open to her, and his opinions, just plain crazy or amazingly insightful, were shared through the *Bay Banner*, the newspaper he'd founded.

Cricket greeted her at the door wearing a gold sequined, sleeveless, scooped down-to-there mini-dress. The sinful, sexy dress highlighted her sister's long blonde curls and the gold strappy stilettos she wore that made her as tall as Honey. "Wow, you look great, Cricket."

"This is how normal women dress for an evening out. Come on in. Momma and Miss Bess have already left."

"Good, I didn't want to have to pass inspection by Grand."

"Tell me something, did you never go out when you lived in Boston?"

"I worked long hours, sometime fourteen hours a day, so at night I kinda collapsed on the couch with a bowl of cashews. But I do have a great black wool suit."

"Which you will never wear here. It's never cold enough to wear wool."

"Right. Let's get this makeover started."

"I have five different dresses for you to try, and then I'll do your makeup. But first a shower, and make sure you wash away any thoughts of Chef Andy, murder, and the Blue Oyster Grill. You're going to look like a million bucks and have fun tonight. Erase killer from your mind."

"Right." But could she wash away a death threat?

"Remember, your eggs are dryin' up."

Honey rolled her eyes and made her way to the upstairs bathroom. She loved this old house with its spacious rooms and high ceilings, Florida pine plank floors, and elaborate hand-carved woodwork. Only the kitchen and first floor bathroom had been updated, the living room, dining and library retained their original paneled and leather furnishings charm. Four bedrooms, the bath, and a veranda-wide sunroom completed the second floor. The attic remained a mystery known only to her mother and Grandma Bess.

Honey took her time, basking in a long, hot shower. If it were possible to wash away her anxiety, the frightening personal death threat, and the horrifying murders for a few hours it might be refreshing to just be. To just be Honey. But how in the world could she do that? Forget the present and revert to the past? Back to when she was sixteen years old again with no worries. To just be Honey, a young girl feeling the music flow through her, dancing freely and wildly, loving the high school hero. *No. No. No.* A fire burned in the pit of her stomach.

As soon as Honey emerged from the shower, an impatient Cricket called, "Come into my room. We've got to hurry."

Tamping down her anxiety, she followed her sister's orders.

Grinning, Cricket held up a strapless red sequined dress. Apparently, her younger sister was obsessed with sequins. "No one will take their eyes off you in this dress."

"Which is not what I'm after." Honey shook her head. "That is just so not me."

Her sister released a heavy sigh which said

everything. "How 'bout this number? It's sophisticated but sexy, royal blue lace, long sleeves, short skirt, and a plunging neckline."

"Did Momma let you wear this dress out of the house?"

"Are you kidding? She's never seen me wearing this dress."

"She's not going to see me wearing it either. I do not plunge, Cricket."

"Moving on, this is one of my favorites, a white crystal beaded halter top with plenty of sexy shoulder exposure and a black crepe mini skirt."

Honey nodded. "This one. I can expose my shoulders." Classic black and white, even though the skirt was short, at least there was no plunging going on. Besides, Honey rationalized, the dress was probably the most conservative of the garments in Cricket's closet, and beggars could not be choosers.

Cricket insisted on styling Honey's hair, wielding a curling iron. "You cannot wear a ponytail with this dress."

Before she knew it, Honey's hair fell in a glossy sun-streaked sheen to her shoulders.

Her sister stood behind her as they both gazed into the mirror. "See what a blow dryer and curling iron can do?" Before Honey could answer, Cricket continued. "Now I'm going to do your makeup. Watch closely."

Honey chuckled and gave Cricket a wink. "Yes, ma'am."

Why hadn't they done this before? Being glamorized was fun and Cricket was in her element, calling the shots for a change.

While her younger sister worked her magic, Honey

speculated on the evening ahead. Would the Bay killer be there? Was the person who left her the threatening message the killer? Would Eli be at the fundraiser tonight? Most likely. Even though he would never love her again, she'd rather dwell on him than the killer. She wanted to shine tonight. If that was even possible. She would like Eli to remember that aside from her thick reporter skin, she remained a desirable woman. She hoped.

"Honey, are you thinking about Chef Andy again?"

"No." For the first time in days, her thoughts were on another man. One very much alive.

"Let's go then. You're done and gorgeous. How did I not know my sister could cleanup so well?"

"If that's the case, no one will recognize me."

Cricket made a face. "Puleeze. Let's go. The timing is right for us to make a spectacular entrance."

"Spectacular?" A word, a condition, so out of Honey's comfort zone.

Since riding her scooter was out of the question, with a bit of trepidation she became Cricket's passenger in her little mini for the three-minute route to the Blue Oyster Bay Senior Citizen's Center.

"We don't want to ruin our hair," Cricket explained, as she peeled out of the driveway.

****

The Lighthouse, the Bay's Senior Center Building, was laid out like a stealth bomber. Two wings stretched back from the center on either side. The right wing contained the rooms and dining area of the residents, and the left wing held the crafts rooms, exercise rooms, music rooms and card room. The lobby and the main hall were located front and center where events like the fundraiser were held. Resident rooms lined the rear corridor.

After paying for their tickets, Honey and Cricket entered the hall. Grandma Bess and her band of sixty-five plus senior musicians were playing a rousing rendition of "Young at Heart". The hall decorations were early nineteen seventies, sparkling silver disco balls dangled from the ceiling and crepe paper draped the bar and serving tables. The tables surrounding the dance floor held heaping platters of chips, peanuts, and processed cheese slices, as well as the twinkling candle votives.

Honey spotted a line at the cash bar in the back of the room. She tugged her skirt down to bring it closer to her knees. Self-conscious, she'd started to sweat.

"You need a glass of wine," Cricket steered Honey toward the bar. "Let's get a drink and mingle."

"Mingle? I hardly know anyone in Blue Oyster Bay anymore besides you and Marylu." But surely a glass of wine, or two, would help soothe her nerves tonight.

Cricket gestured to the dance floor. "Marylu's over there, dancing with Eric Dunlap."

Honey nodded vaguely. "I'll grab a chardonnay and sit for a minute." She pointed to an empty table against the wall where she could get a good view of everyone in the hall and those entering.

"You are not going to be a wallflower," Cricket declared.

"Well, no…"

"You need to show Eli what he's missing."

"I'll be at the table. He'll see me," Honey grumbled.

"Henry's my date tonight. We'll sit together."

"Is he bringing a friend?"

"Yes."

Honey raised her gaze heavenward. "Why am I not surprised?"

Once seated and clutching her wine as if it were a lifeline, she scanned the crowd. Her mother and Miss Bess were chatting with the President of the Blue Oyster Bay Women's Guild. She didn't see Thea and Carol, but then she hadn't expected them to be here. Rachel and Ace were also among the missing. Since none of her suspects were in attendance, Honey had nothing to do but relax and attempt to enjoy herself. Which seemed an impossible task. Within thirty minutes, Henry and Leo had joined the table with Cricket and Honey. Cricket had arranged for Leo to be Honey's date. Annoyed more than she could say until she and her sister were alone, Honey made another visit to the bar. In order to get through this evening, she required copious glasses of wine.

Sipping her second glass of chardonnay at the table, she jumped and spilled a bit when Leo shouted, "There's my boss!"

Honey followed Leo's gaze to the dance floor. Eli and Krystal were dancing. There didn't seem to be any conversation between them, but there didn't need to be. In Honey's eyes, Krystal looked like a goddess in a long, figure-clinging formal gown of scarlet, slit up the side and strapless, revealing an enviable amount of cleavage.

Honey couldn't just sit and watch like a child with her nose pressed up against the window, longing for something she couldn't have. Pushing her chair back, she stood. "Leo…let's dance."

"What?"

"Let's dance. Now," Honey insisted beneath her breath.

His eyes lit up. "Okay."

Once on the dance floor Honey relaxed a bit, enveloped by the crowd, determined to lose herself in the music and avoid the sight of Krystal clinging to Eli's body. The image of the couple slow dancing body-to-body shouldn't disturb her. But it did. It was as if a gory crime scene were happening right in front of her. She kept Leo at a distance. Nausea swirled in her belly. A knot lodged in her throat. When the dance ended, she sought escape.

"Thanks, Leo. Great dance but I…I just need a little fresh air." She rushed away, out the French doors leading to the balcony and onto the slate patio. Once in the open air, Honey could make her getaway. She had a plan. Slip off her shoes, walk to her family home, change her clothes, and take off on her scooter. She would be home before anyone noticed she'd gone.

The cool, salty night air felt soothing. Nature's tranquility served as a cure to nerves, fear, sadness, and love lost. All the emotions she struggled to suppress. Inside the ballroom she'd felt stifled, smothered almost. Out in the evening air, she could breathe again. Slipping off Cricket's stilettos, she slowly strolled to the railing overlooking the bay. The full silver moon shone on the dancing waves. She gazed out over the endless water while a thousand stars sparkled above her. The stars were never this bright in Boston, the air never this fresh.

"You're not planning to jump, are you?"

She did jump—in place. Eli's deep rumble startled her, but his tone wasn't austere as usual, it even held a hint of amusement.

Honey turned to him as he sidled up beside her. "No." she grinned. "You can't be rid of me that easily."

"I don't want to be rid of you. But I am interested in why you're with Leo tonight."

"Leo? I'm not with Leo."

"You were dancing with him, sitting at the table with him. Are you trying to pry classified information from my deputy?"

"No." She shook her head. "No. I'm here to support the fundraiser and Grandma Bess. Cricket arranged for Leo to be at our table."

"Miss Bessie is a mighty fine piano player."

"Yes, she is." Honey's stomach tumbled with tension. Eli stood too close. His voice was too soft and…and friendly. His spicy aftershave filled her senses. Her hands trembled.

"I forgot to ask if you got your raccoon problem fixed."

"Yes, they're gone." *But I have no idea what to do about the death threat. Should I tell you?*

"Despite the uninvited wildlife, you're livin' in a sweet spot. Done any more work on the beach house?"

"No," she admitted softly. "I haven't had much time, but I have unpacked some boxes." *Were they having a conversation? A real conversation? Every breath she took was filled with Eli. His deep woods scent, his masculinity. His deliciousness.*

"Does that mean you've decided to stay in Oyster Bay?" he asked.

She shrugged. "Means…I guess…that I've unpacked more boxes."

He nodded.

No, she wouldn't tell him about the death threat. If she wanted Eli's attention, she wanted it to be from his heart, not his badge. Oh, my dear lord, did she really just think that?

"How's your dad?" she asked. "Momma told me just today that Bill was a resident here. I'm so sorry. I didn't know."

"Some days he's good and remembers a bit, some days he's not, roams like a lost soul."

"It must be difficult for you. If I had known—"

"He's been this way awhile. Dad has a couple of medical problems as well as the dementia."

"I'm sorry," she repeated. Feeling awkward and uncomfortable, inexplicable heat burned on the back of her neck.

"We're able to take care of his heart with medication but…" Eli's voice trailed off.

"Bill's a good man and you've always been a good son. He's lucky to have you."

"Appreciate hearing that. Not everyone is so kind."

"Maybe they've forgotten the man he used to be."

"Before the drinking?"

"Even after. You know, I didn't have much time with my dad—but Bill—I remember that Bill always gave me a hug when I needed one. He would just know. He's a good, loving man."

"With a problem." Eli sighed and seemed to talk to the night, to the bay. "An addiction. A disease. I'm glad I came back to the Bay when I did. We shared a few good years before the dementia got bad. And being here now so I can take care of him feels good too. Despite his alcoholism, which began when Mom left, he took care of me growing up. As best he could. Couldn't have been easy for him."

"You were the high school hero. I don't remember you ever being in any trouble. You never gave your dad a reason to worry."

His lips turned up in a rueful smile. "Didn't have time, I guess."

Smiling, gazing out to sea, Honey nodded. "No, you just studied and played ball."

"And took my girlfriend to the beach."

"She…she…those times were happy times for her," Honey murmured. "For your girlfriend. Those days might have been the happiest times in her life." How odd, she thought, they were talking to the sea. Not looking at each other, but out across the bay. They talked about the past, about each other, about feelings yet naming no names. Halting, painful…promising.

"Good to know." He paused, cleared his throat, and spoke quietly, as if to himself. "Not all memories are bad when you think about them after a time. After a certain amount of time has passed."

And your emotions are no longer raw? "You're right. I…I have the best memories a woman could have," she added in a rush. "And for the record, Eli Gibson, you've been the best son a man could ever want."

He turned, looked down on her. "Thank you." The warmth of his smile gave Honey goose bumps.

"And you were always a great date."

"Yeah." He chuckled. Actually chuckled.

It almost felt like a romantic moment. Almost. Honey's heart leapt into overdrive. Her knees wobbled precariously. She might be in danger of falling from the balcony into the bay below. How to stop the fall? Stop her madness? A change of subject. "Eli, speaking of dates, yours, Krystal, looks beautiful tonight. I'm assuming you two are a…a hot item?"

"That's what the Bay gossip line calls us." He

nodded. A grave expression came over him as he stared down into the bay. "And well, it's time for me to be starting a family if I'm ever gonna have one."

"You're still a young man. You're only a year or two older than me." *And yet her family reminded Honey daily that her eggs were drying up.*

"It's time for me to settle down. It's time if I want to be taking my son fishing, hiking." A wistful smile settled at the corner of his mouth as Eli imagined the future aloud. "I want to explore Dog Island with my boy and do all the other dad and son stuff my dad used to do with me in the early days."

Honey shared Eli's vision; she envisioned a blue-eyed, freckled-face boy holding fast to his hand. "You will. You'll still be doing all those things when you're a senior citizen."

"Yeah." He cleared his throat as if he was clearing away his lapse into sentiment. "What about you? Are you ever going to be ready to settle down?"

"I…I don't know." She could not face him. Could not look into his eyes.

"Never remember you sayin' you wanted kids, a family."

"Well, but…of course I do." The moment she replied, she knew it to be true. Becoming a mother, having a family was a given just like being a journalist was a given, a part of her. "It's just never been the right time."

Again, he nodded, swept a hand through his hair. "Hope you find your right time, before it passes you by."

And my eggs dry up. She thought.

"There you are!" Krystal's octave high voice cut through the quiet night like a knife.

Eli turned.

"I've been looking all over for you, my handsome Sheriff." Ignoring Honey, Eli's date slipped an arm through his.

"Sorry, Kris. I was just doin' a bit of business with the *Banner's* star reporter."

She turned, aiming a way too sweet smile at Honey. "Hello again, Miss Mayhew."

"Hello "

"If you don't mind, I'm going to steal the sexiest man in town away from you." Her smile was warm, but her eyes were colder than a glacier. "Eli and I have some more dancing to do."

Honey forced a smile, nodded. She raised her gaze to Eli's. "Of course. Have a good time. Make happy memories."

"Goodnight, Honey."

Eli had called her Honey. He'd said her name, barely a murmur, before tearing his gaze away and turning from her.

She did not watch him leave. Honey gazed up at the moon and felt the warmth of its glow. Her heart swelled with hope. Alone together for the first time since she'd returned, she and Eli hadn't discussed the murders or a killer. For the first time they'd been true to each other. Except for that one little omission. She hadn't told him about the death threat. She hadn't told him that her life might be in danger.

Chapter 11

Honey made an Irish exit from the fundraiser. Under cover of darkness, she slipped on her shoes and fled from the balcony. An SOS text to Cricket resulted in a ride back to her sister's and her scooter without too many questions.

But she didn't miss the rather smug smile on her sister's face when she said, "I know you and Eli were out on the balcony together. I know you still care for him, and Eli still cares for you."

"Stop it. Stop thinking things like that. Stop saying things like that."

"Oh, did I say it aloud?"

"You know nothing. Thinking, saying it, does not make it so." *Nor did wishing it.* Immediately a wave of remorse swept through her. She hadn't meant to snap at Cricket.

Thirty minutes later, the warm sense of contentment Honey had felt with Eli—at least that's what she thought she felt—contentment had never been her best friend, ended. A case of serious shakes set in when she reached home. She'd left no lights on in the beach house and the threat to her life she'd left undeleted on her computer returned in a rush. The threat flashed in her mind like a neon sign to push all thoughts of Eli from her mind. The darkened beach house appeared daunting, even dangerous in the dim moonlight.

A chill snaked down her spine. The warm, humid night air closed in on her, stealing her breath away. And then she spotted him.

Panting heavily, Fred watched for her from the top of the stairs. As he always did.

Once again, she'd let her imagination run rampant. No one waited to kill her. This was Blue Oyster Bay. After taking several deep breaths, her nerves soothed. Still, Honey talked to Fred all the way up the steps. "Hey, boy. No problems here, right? You'd bark, maybe bite, if someone tried to get into the house, right?"

Wrong. Fred would lick an intruder to death.

"Besides, I'm armed," she boomed, just in case someone was lurking in her rental.

True enough, she had a right arm and a left arm.

Pausing at the door, Honey jangled her keys loudly as a warning for anyone lying in wait for her. Heart racing, she burst through the door and flicked on the light switch. The kitchen, living and dining areas flooded with light. Dashing from room to room, she did not stop until the house was ablaze with light. To her vast relief, no one screamed or leaped out at her. Taking no chances and just to be sure, she retraced her steps, searching every nook and cranny where an intruder might lurk.

Drooling, Fred followed her, sniffing loudly.

The old dog probably thought her a maniac. He might be on to something.

Satisfied she was alone in the beach house, Honey sat down and turned on the computer. The threatening email message wasn't there. It had disappeared. *What?*

Had she deleted the warning by mistake? Or had she only imagined the message had been there at all, so caught up in her Bay Killer story that she'd made herself a part of the crime drama? Had she hallucinated, or had she become obsessed? Tears blurred her vision. What the heck? Ambition might become the death of her yet.

Honey pressed any and all keys that might restore the message, to no avail. It did not exist. Her eyes burned with tears of frustration.

She shut down the computer.

Determined to clear her mind and soothe her nerves, she dove into pure physical labor. After changing into her pajamas, Honey slapped on Eli's old baseball cap and emptied three more boxes before she felt tired enough to drag her body to bed. After tossing and turning for several hours, she finally slept. Sort of.

She dreamed of being strangled by a stranger wearing a fright mask. Eli came to her rescue, tall, dark, handsome, and daunting. He would save her; his resolute expression told her so. The sheriff still loved her. But when Honey flew into his arms seeking comfort, needing love, he evaporated. His figure dissolved in her arms like a sugar soldier in the rain.

She woke with a start, with empty arms, her body tangled in the sheets in a cold sweat.

Not now. Not Eli. Not dreams. Fully awake now with the house lights still on and the sun blasting through the windows, she shook off the distractions of her meandering mind. She had a murder story to write, and as of now it had way too many loose ends. For the first time in her working life, Honey was going to be late for work.

Grandma Bess was waiting for her when Honey hurried into the *Banner Bay* office an hour later with barely a nod. If she could just slip into her computer station her mother might not notice her late arrival.

But Miss Bess was prepared to chat. "We raised a thousand dollars for the Lighthouse, Shuga."

"Awesome!" She was duly impressed at the generosity of the impoverished little coastal town. No matter what was going on in the rest of the world, the residents of the small panhandle town took care of their own.

"Ah'm gonna help you write the article."

"Thanks, Grand. You are the expert on the senior citizen's center."

"Gotta talk to you first, Shuga."

"Okay." Honey stopped, frowned, concerned with the older woman's appearance. Grandma Bess wore no makeup. Her naked face was deeply lined and flecked with the telling brown spots of age. Her bright orange hair hadn't been brushed. Something was wrong. She looked as if she fell out of bed and came directly to the *Banner Bay* office. "Has something happened?"

"Not here. Walk with me." She tucked an arm through Honey's as she slowly hobbled through the back door, head down, shoulders hunched. Where was her head-held-high grandmother? What had happened to the unbreakable woman she knew?

Miss Bess steered her to an old wooden bench on a nearby dock. From time to time, Honey glanced over her shoulder. The shrimp boats had left for the day and there was no one in sight. Still, she couldn't help but wonder how long she would be looking over her shoulder to make certain she wasn't being followed. By a killer.

Honey circled an arm around her grandmother's shoulders. "Miss Bess, are you all right?"

She shook her head. "No."

"What's wrong?"

She shook her head again. When she looked up at Honey her eyes shone with tears.

Familiar angst choked Honey. Grand's cancer had returned, or her boyfriend had died. "Tell me what's happened. What's wrong, Miss Bess?"

"It's silly."

"Nothing that upsets my grand is silly. Let's go back to the office. I'll make you some tea and I could use another cup of coffee."

"He broke it off."

"What?"

"Stanley. He said he couldn't take it anymore. He dumped me."

"What?" Honey repeated.

Miss Bess slowly nodded. "He said he was torn between two women, his daughter and me."

"Oh, no. And so he broke it off with you?"

"Why can't his daughter understand? Old people need love too. It's a fact. We live longer if we have companionship." She paused, batting back her tears. "That's a fact too."

"Of course. Oh, Miss Bess, I'm so sorry. I know how much he means to you."

"Stanley and ah…" Her grandmother dissolved into heart wrenching sobs.

Honey's heart broke for her. Pain remembered pierced like a knife. "Stanley will come back to you," she assured the family matriarch. "He'll very quickly understand what a mistake he's made."

"His daughter is worse than a witch," Miss Bess hissed.

"No question about it." Anyone who caused her grandmother to cry was worse than a bitch. "Karma will get her in the end."

"Ah hope so. Afraid ah'm going to move into her mother's house, his house, she told Stanley."

"I thought her mother passed."

"She did. Bless her heart. Seven years ago."

"Do you want to move into Stanley's house?"

"Good lord, no. She told Stanley that first ah'd move in and then ah'd be taking his money. Have him sign papers, sign the house and his money away."

Icy outrage, glacier-sized, surged through Honey. "That's a grade B movie plot! I've seen that movie a hundred times. Do you want me to talk with her?" Before Grandma Bess could answer, Honey made a decision. "I'll talk with her."

"No. The witch lives all the way up to the next county."

"Miss Bess, you deserve better. From Stanley and from his daughter."

The old woman cocked her head, wiped her eyes. "Ah do, ah do, don't I?"

"You certainly do. He should be defending you, not breaking up with you and breaking your heart. Stanley's daughter needs to learn a lesson in love." *As more than likely did Honey.*

Miss Bess swiped her tears away with the back of her hand. "That's a fact. It's not like we have all the time in the world. At our age the insurance companies classify us as elderly, ya know. Any one of us could croak tomorrow."

"No. No, you're not going to croak any time soon. Don't say that."

"Sugha, let's be real." She paused and took a deep breath. "Ah have more yesterdays than tomorrows."

"Stanley isn't the only man at the senior center," Honey reminded her.

Miss Bess nodded, pursed her lips. Her eyes sparked with their normal feistiness. "But he's the most fun. Ah used to like George, but he got so cranky. The rheumatoid got to him and stole his sense of humor."

"We'll find someone else for you."

"We'll see. Ah just may get a dog."

Fred? Did her grandmother have eyes on Fred? No, Honey realized she'd grown too attached to the old drooly dog. She'd get her grandmother a puppy. Except a pup might not do for a woman Grand Bess's age. An excellent alternative beckoned. A shopping trip to take her mind off her breaking heart, if only for a while. Grand loved clothes. And she wore them well. "Miss Bess, we're going to Port St. Georges right now and buying a new wardrobe. We are going to dazzle the new men in our lives."

"Do you have a new man, Honey?" Grandma Bess blinked her eyes in confusion. "There are no new men to be had that Ah know of."

"That could change in a minute." *If only.*

"What about writing your story?"

"It won't take me long. While I'm writing you go fix yourself up. Just in case. You don't want to chance Stanley seeing you in…in disarray. We just have to make one stop on the way."

Thirty minutes later Honey drove Miss Bess's car into the parking lot at the sheriff's office.

Her grandmother frowned. "What are we doing here?"

"Gathering information for my next story."

"Which story?"

"Someone has to write about not one, but two unexpected deaths in town. Chef Andy and Donald Turner. That's odd for the Bay, you've got to admit."

Miss Bess cast a dubious frown Honey's way. "Or is that your excuse for seein' the sheriff? You keep after Eli and you know, you'll catch him."

Honey felt a buzz of irritation. "I'm not stalking the sheriff," she assured Miss Bess more defensively than she meant to. "This is business. There is a real story here. My conversations with Eli are purely professional. Please wait in the car. I'll be right back."

"If you say so." And then Miss Bess did something she rarely did. She *tsked*. Just like an old woman.

Honey squared her shoulders and hurried into the police office. Relieved to find Leo alone, Honey smiled brightly. "Good morning."

"Honey. Where'd you go last night? I was worried."

"Didn't Cricket explain? The world's worst headache came over me. And well, I didn't want to spoil your fun by being a party pooper."

"You could never be that."

She shot him an apologetic smile. "Please forgive me?"

"No worries."

"I just popped in for a minute. Miss Bess is waiting in her car for me."

"What can I do for you? Sort of busy here this morning. The town council has asked Eli to run for mayor."

Taken by surprise, Honey gasped, "Really? That seems an unexpected honor from the good old boys of Blue Oyster Bay. Is he going to run?"

Leo shrugged. "The last candidate's body isn't even

cold yet."

"Right. Don Turner." A lump of oyster-sized fear clogged Honey's throat. Although he was sheriff, she'd never considered Eli in any danger. Eli was what every man wanted to be, big, strong, and smart. He knew how to stay safe. Didn't he?

Leo snapped Honey out of her musing. "If you've come to see Eli, sorry to say he's not here."

Distracted, she nodded, her mind still swirling with thoughts of Eli as Mayor of the Bay. "Just answer one quick question. Has the autopsy come in on Turner yet?"

"Blunt trauma."

"He didn't drown?"

"That came after." Leo said.

A deep voice rumbled from behind her. "Turner was dumped into the river unconscious but alive."

Her heart stopped. "Eli."

"'Course he could have fallen, hit his head and rolled into the bay." Eli strode by her to his desk. "I was about to call you."

"What a horrible way for him to die." A wave of sorrow swept through her for the lawyer.

"Yeah." He nodded as his gaze met hers.

She read speculation in his dark eyes. "I, I was in the neighborhood. I mean that's why I stopped by."

"And you just thought you'd ask Leo a few questions?"

"Actually, I hoped you'd be here." Her cheeks grew warm. It was true, she'd been hoping to see him and confirm the new state of friendship they'd achieved the night before.

"Well, now I am. Anything else you want to know?"

He was all business now. Last night, forgotten. But

yes, Honey wanted to know if he was seriously considering a run for mayor. But now wasn't the time. She nodded, assuming her all-business persona. "Do you have any ideas who could be behind these…deaths? Is Turner's death connected to Andy?"

"No ideas at the moment, and I don't know if there's any connection. It's early in the investigation." His deep blue eyes met hers for a lightening moment before he sank into the chair behind his desk. "I'll call you if I learn anything."

She'd been dismissed. Honey chewed on her lip, torn. Would he call?

"Is there something else on your mind, Honey?"

Yes, many. I received a death threat, and I don't want to die like Andy or Don Turner. And I want to know if you're going to be a mayoral candidate. My questions call for a one-on-one interview in a quiet, secluded place.

"Honey?"

"No. No, Miss Bess is waiting in the car for me. We're going shopping."

He gave her half-grin. "Getting out of town for a bit will do you good. Have fun."

"Thanks." Was that a friendly comment or a sign of relief that she'd be out of town for a minute? Flashing him a smile and thankful he did not seem disturbed by her unexpected appearance, Honey hurried out of his office.

****

Eli watched Honey as she made her way to Miss Bessie's little bug of a car. She hadn't changed much. Her figure remained the same as when they'd been in school, alluring in a willowy sort of way. She didn't have abundant boobs, a tiny waist, or full hips, but somehow her body seemed perfect. Rounded in the right places.

He couldn't take his eyes off her. Bound in a ponytail, the blond strands of her hair glistened in the morning sun. And minutes ago, when her gaze had met his, he saw the intelligence she'd always possessed glint in her eyes. He thought he'd caught a flicker of pain there too but blamed it on his imagination. His ego demanded that Honey still regretted their breakup all those years ago. That she still felt the hurt that he did.

What would she think of him becoming mayor? Would she care? Would she campaign for him if he decided to run? Hell, more than likely she didn't think of him at all beyond the story, the deaths of Andy Mueller and Don Turner.

Honey still possessed that intensity, the old, ingrained ambition that had destroyed the future they'd planned together. When she got the story she wanted in Blue Oyster Bay, Honey would be gone. Eli knew it, felt it in his gut. Otherwise, he'd be in danger of letting himself go and fall crashing, tumbling, headlong in love with her. Again. In so many ways the professional woman she flaunted, the hell-bent reporter of today, reminded him of the intense Honey he'd loved. Yesterday. The girl who challenged him at every turn, loved him unconditionally. Or so he'd thought.

****

Honey's heart was still pounding when she reached the car. The old reaction to being within three feet of Eli had returned. The old reaction wasn't necessarily a good reaction. It was distracting. She pasted on a smile for her grandmother, who was experiencing her own heart problems at the moment. They were going to have a good time this afternoon no matter what!

Honey started the car, which slowly rumbled and grumbled to life.

But her mind wasn't ready to leave the distracting sheriff. Her grand was wrong. Eli would never take her back. And if by chance he did, reconciling would mean she couldn't leave Blue Oyster Bay. She would be trapped. She would end up living here forever, loving Eli, and raising their babies. The scenario gave her a jolt. The scene playing out in her mind had played there before. Long ago. It wasn't new. It was deja vu, an old high school dream, before she got caught up in ambition. It was definitely not the dream she'd been working for all of these years. Not at all. She vaguely wondered if it was time to dream a new dream. Or return to an old dream? C.S. Lewis once wrote that you were never too old to dream a new dream.

"Are you ready Miss Bess? We're off to Stewart's to get ourselves a glamorous wardrobe."

"I want the kinds of things Cricket wears."

Honey chuckled. "Grand, you'd be arrested!"

Undaunted, her grandmother replied, "You could use some of her style too."

"Maybe." *Maybe in pursuit of reporting success she'd been neglecting the woman girly-girly inside for too long.*

Thirty-five minutes later, Honey pulled into the Stewart Department Store parking lot. Stewarts was the largest closest shopping mecca for Oyster Bay residents. Tallahassee was more than an hour's drive away and Honey felt better being closer to home.

They'd barely arrived in the women's section when Miss Bess disappeared into a fitting room with half a dozen new outfits in her favorite purple color. Honey's job was to approve or disapprove each as her grandmother modeled for her, complete with twirls, in a private fashion show.

The first short, flirty-hemmed dress her grandmother tried on was definitely designed for a twenty-year old but looked oddly attractive on her. the seventy-five-year-old. "No man will be able to resist you in that dress, Miss Bess."

"That's the plan, Sugha. And you know, you're right about Stanley."

"Maybe, but I've been having second thoughts. If I can't talk to his daughter, I may just have to have a heart-to-heart with Stanley."

"Oh, Sugha, no."

But yes, that's what Honey decided to do. If she couldn't straighten out her own love life, she was determined to have better luck with her grandmother's.

An hour later, clutching three outfits as if someone might snatch them away, Miss Bess checked out. "Honey, you go on over to the young lady section and get yourself something short and sexy."

"Short and sexy just isn't me."

"Short and sexy lives inside every woman, and you'd better find yours before your eggs dry up completely, Sugha."

Giving her grand a short moan in response, Honey wandered over to the section marked, "Hot to Trot."

A summer dress caught her eye: the long skirt meant she could wear it on her scooter and remain decent. As she pulled the gauzy, pastel rainbow frock from the rack and held it up, a movement across the room begged her attention. *Whaaat?*

Carol Kahn and Thea Mueller. The two were giggling like teenagers out on a shopping spree. Each woman held at least three bags as they headed for the door. Apparently, the bags held new wardrobes for the widow and her best friend, both of whom looked happier than Honey had seen either of them in weeks. Neither woman appeared to be in mourning.

Was it normal for a grieving widow to go shopping? Honey hated herself for wondering, for being suspicious, but she was. Were the women spending the impending insurance money gained by Chef Andy's murder? Was Thea a killer? Or was it Carol? Or were they partners in crime? How could they be so happy? Were they planning a trip out of town on the ruse of taking a vacation? Away from the Bay and prying eyes. Okay, Honey's prying eyes.

Confusion caused her head to ache. The women appeared so different, so care-free. Or were they simply reeling from release, a release from the despair of death?

"Did you find something?" Miss Bess asked, sidling up to Honey.

"I may have," she mumbled, eyeing Thea and Carol.

But the women left the store, and she was in no position to follow them. But she would have if she could have.

"Put that ice cream cone dress down," her grandmother scolded. "Ah've found just the thing for you. It's in mah bag. Let's go. Ah need to do some thinkin'."

Honey reluctantly tore her mind away from the widow and her friend. "Thinking about what?"

"Which of mah widower bachelor friends to make a play for wearin' my brand-new knock-your-socks-off

156

dresses. Mah legs are still good, you know."

"I know, Grand, you've got great legs."

"And Ah'm going to enjoy watching Stanley go green with jealousy when Ah'm with another man."

"I'd like to see that too."

"It's an old school strategy you might consider with Eli."

"Eli? No." *Jealous? No way. She'd never known him to be jealous when they were together.*

"Now that's somethin' to think about Sugha."

But Honey felt she had much more important things to think about. What was behind Thea's swift recovery from grieving widow to giggling shopper? The spouse was always the first suspect. Had Eli thoroughly investigated Thea's alibi?

"Um…I will." She needed to talk to the sheriff. Now.

"And just watch me at the Collins Brothers Concert this Saturday night. Ahm gonna look super-hot in mah new dance dress."

"Um hum."

"Did you hear a word Ah said?"

"Um…" Honey's mind was on Thea and Carol. "What? A concert?"

"Every year we close off Main Street and have a block party when the Collins brothers come to town. They're hometown boys, you know."

Honey shook her head. "The Bay is a lot busier than I remember."

"Always somethin' goin' on, and if there isn't, well, you make somethin' happen."

"A block party and concert," Honey murmured. *On top of two murders and a death threat. What else could happen?*

"And you're goin' with me in the new dress your Grand just bought for you."

"Oh, no." Honey shuttered to think what could be in her grandmother's bag for her.

"Oh, yes."

The last thing Honey wanted to do was run into Eli with Krystal again. And the happy couple would surely be at the concert. Eli would be everywhere from now on, looking for killers or running for mayor. She could not un-see him dancing with Krystal at the senior center fundraiser, a perfect couple, one handsome man and his drop-dead gorgeous woman. They looked like they belonged together, a model couple gazing at you from the pages of a glossy magazine or smiling down from a billboard on Highway 98.

Her stomach churned.

"Ah happen to know your momma is assignin' you the concert story. You're goin' to the concert."

Another crowd. Another night of looking over her shoulder. Another round of sweaty palms and heart palpitations. She couldn't wait.

Chapter 12

Although Honey'd hoped with every fiber of her being, almost to a prayer, that the Collins Concert would be rained out, the perfect night arrived.

A gentle evening breeze blew skirts up and soothing salt air into every breath she took. A golden crescent moon and a multitude of silver stars shone on the crowd. A perfect night for another murder?

The entire block had been closed off to traffic, which allowed for a makeshift outdoor venue. A stage of sorts rose in the center of Main Street complete with blinking, colored lights, and sound equipment. Wrought iron cafe tables and chairs lined each side of the street with additional folding chairs arranged in the middle of the street. But unless you had clout, the concert appeared to be standing room only with an hour to go before the music started.

Honey found Cricket, camera slung around her neck, sitting with Miss Bess at a table for two. Cricket wore her usual uniform of mini skirt and strapless top with a skin-full gap between the brief top and the waist of the skirt. Momma must not have seen her leave the house.

Miss Bess's outfit boasted a green, gauzy blouse whose sleeves floated in the breeze. Her forest green palazzo pants featured a wow factor of sexy side slits up to the knees. Her tangerine curls were piled atop her head and her lips were painted a vampire red. Honey chuckled. Grand Bess gave her granddaughters a run for their makeup money.

Honey had had no choice; she wore the dress her grandmother had given her. The powder-blue chiffon-y halter style dress flowed and swished to a stop a good three inches above her knees. She'd brushed her sun-streaked mane to a shiny mass and released it from its usual ponytail rubber band to fall in a bit of a tangle to her shoulders. For good measure she'd added mascara, gloss, and a splash of blush.

"Ah love your new look, Sugha."

"Yeah," Cricket agreed, giving Honey the once-over. "What happened to you?"

Honey grabbed Cricket by the hand and pulled her out of her chair. "Come with me. Grandma Bess, whatever you do, do not leave this table and your chair. You'll never find another."

Miss Bess nodded vaguely, apparently searching the crowd for someone she knew to sit with her. She couldn't be alone.

"Cricket and I are going to get the pictures for the story and be right back. This won't take long." And then Honey was going home.

But a few feet away from Miss Bess, Cricket stopped. "Wait."

"What?"

"I've something to tell you."

"What?"

"Last night, on my way home from my class, I was nearly driven off the road."

Honey's heart dropped to her toes. "What!"

"I was so scared, I'm still shaking." Cricket held up

a shaky hand to demonstrate. "What kind of nutcase plays chicken on a rainy night?"

"I don't know. I don't know. What did you do?" She could barely breathe with the thought she might have lost her sister.

"I closed my eyes and side-swiped-slammed the jerk's car. Take the offensive, Miss Bess always says."

"Cricket! You could have been killed!" Honey's stomach flipped in a nauseating tumble.

"Don't I know!" Her amber eyes widened.

"What kind of car was it?"

"A black truck." Her squeaky voice reached a hitherto unknown high note. "I don't know what make. I don't know cars. The last I saw it was headed toward a tree on the forest side."

"Oh my God."

"I know, right?" She let out a heavy breath. "I sped away. Just in case they called the cops."

Wavering in shock, Honey quietly asked, "You're saying you didn't report almost being killed?"

"No."

"Someone might have been hurt, or killed, in the other car."

"I don't think so. I drove by the spot this morning and the truck wasn't there. Guess I would have heard by now if the maniac, the driver, had reported the, ah, collision."

"You're sure you're all right? No whiplash or anything."

"I'm fine. But I'll kill the truck driver if I ever find him. Or her."

"It might have been a tourist, long gone by now," Honey said. Hoped. Was the threat to Cricket's life even meant for her? Or could it have been meant to warn Honey to get out of town now? Did the jerk, i.e., killer, who attempted to run Cricket off the road frighten the wrong woman, thinking Cricket was Honey driving? Or were they determined to hurt anyone in her family in order to put pressure on her? The sickening sensation in her belly got worse. She was on the verge of throwing up. It could not be. It could not be all about her.

"Thanks for letting me vent. I was afraid if I told Mom or Miss Bess that I'd get a lecture."

"What about reporting to the sheriff?"

"He's got enough on his plate without worrying about a traffic incident."

"But what if it wasn't a traffic—"

"I feel like dancing," Cricket interrupted with a bright smile. "I need to let loose and forget it. So let's go shoot those pictures now."

"Good idea." Except that Honey couldn't let loose or forget the dangerous incident. She had to protect her sister, her family from whoever was threatening them. She had to find the black truck and Chef Andy and Turner's murderer. It was up to her. Eli wasn't moving fast enough.

Except she was stuck. She couldn't leave innocent Cricket and Miss Bess alone in this crowd. Frustrated, an edgy restlessness ricocheted through her body.

"Let it go." Cricket's words echoed in her brain. "Let it go."

Distraction. Honey required a momentary distraction. Surveying the crowd, she saw Eli threading through a group of teenagers before he saw her. With the confidence her new, sexy outfit gave her, she stepped in front of him. "Eli, I didn't expect to see you here."

His first reaction was a startled expression. His second action was to blatantly look her over from satin stilettos to her glossy peach lips. "I make all the town events."

"There seem to be more than I remember."

He laughed. "Every week the town celebrates something. We have the Seafood Festival coming up, Founders Day, and Oysters Only Day. You'll need a calendar to keep up. If you stay, that is."

"I have no plans to leave the Bay." *Not yet, anyway.*

"You look…different tonight…in a good way," he added hastily.

"I'll take that as a compliment and keep my grandmother on as my fashion stylist."

He nodded, a half-smile curving the lips she once knew so well. Soft and arousing. "Definitely," he agreed. "Miss Bessie's talents are off the charts. Although my bet would have been on you, Cricket."

Cricket gave him a conspiratorial wink. "Thanks. I have tried." She glanced from Eli to Honey and back. "Um, I'll just be off to the bandstand to take a few pictures while they set up."

Honey called after her sister, "I'll catch up with you in a minute." Turning back to Eli, she asked, "How's your dad doing?"

He shrugged. "Okay. Some days are better than others."

"You see him every day." She made it a statement rather than a question.

"Of course."

Honey chewed on her lip, wondering if now was the time she should confide in him about Cricket's close encounter, the threat to her, and her suspicions. But no.

Not in the middle of a personal conversation. There hadn't been enough of those. "I'll be visiting him from now on too. Now, that I know. I loved your dad, Eli."

"I feel I should warn you. Dad may not remember your name, or actually recognize you, but having another visitor will do his old heart good."

"I hope so." Honey made a show of checking out the crowd. "Where's Krystal tonight?"

"She didn't come down this weekend. Her mother's sick, a summer cold."

"Oh. I'm sorry." *Not.*

"Nothing to be sorry about. I can take care of myself."

"Fending off the Bay's single women."

He grinned. And her heart banged against her chest. "Being a bachelor is sorta like having a target on your back," he said.

She knew about having a target on her back. "But you're not just any bachelor. You're the sheriff. And you played in the major leagues. You're an extraordinary bachelor."

"You forgot to mention how good-looking I am."

She laughed. "Yes, you are. You're still very hot, Eli."

"And I didn't think you noticed."

He was flirting with her, and she was flirting back. It was as if they were back in high school and yet Honey did not know how to handle the unexpected banter. No easy retort sprung to mind. Her throat dried up and her cheeks felt warm. "I totally get why you feel like there's a target on your back. You're a chick magnet, like it or not."

"Is that why you seem always to be where I am."

Embarrassed and barely able to suppress her smile, she hung her head. "I am not stalking you, if that's what you mean. Part of my job is to always know where the sheriff is and what he's thinking."

"You're stalking a story."

"Exactly, but if I weren't I would…" *Oh no, bite your tongue, Honey! What did you almost say? Almost.*

"Are you saying you would be magnetized by my great charm and…good looks?"

She choked. "Obviously…I, I have been…I am a fan. Still. You are a …an amazing man. I never said you weren't. You, you always will be." She was as flustered as a teenager.

He grinned, seeming to take pleasure in how she squirmed. "Friends for life."

"Of course. I'd…I'd like that."

"Or as long as you stay in Blue Oyster Bay."

"I have no immediate plans to leave."

He nodded. "Speaking of friends, do you remember the Collins brothers?"

"Should I?"

"Rick Collins was my pal in school. He played shortstop on the high school team."

"So if he hung out with you I really should remember, but I'm not good with names. Better with faces. If I see him, I'm sure I'll remember."

"Most likely. As I recall you don't forget much."

"Is that another compliment?"

He laughed. Eyes crinkled, his heart-stopping expression appeared both relaxed and amused. "What am I thinking?"

"Well, don't stop."

"Have to. Hate to leave you now, but I gotta catch

up with Rick before the concert starts. You should hang out with us after the performance."

"Right. That would be great." But as he turned to leave, disappointment filled the pit of her stomach, heavy as a brick. She wouldn't see him later and she hadn't mentioned Cricket's being run off the road. She was allowing her feelings to trump her judgement. Later. Later she'd share what had happened with him.

"And Honey, thanks for not mentioning the investigation. It will go better between us if you don't try to help me. You just do your job and I do mine. Don't you think?"

No, she didn't think. And tonight she wouldn't be telling him what she knew.

Sadly and woefully disconcerting, Eli's departure left her feeling lonely in the midst of the crowd. Making her way to the stage, she grabbed Cricket and they set out to find Grand who oddly enough was still sitting where they'd left her. But she wasn't alone. Miss Bess was accompanied by a dapper older man.

"Honey, Cricket, meet mah friend Tommy."

"Hello, Tommy." Miss Bess's evening capture was bald and portly, and gazed at Grand as if she'd just hung the moon. Honey was becoming more convinced that age made no difference when it came to romance. Everyone wanted-no-needed a hug.

"Tommy comes to the Senior Center to play Bingo three times a week."

"Are you a winner?" Cricket asked.

"Naw, not at Bingo," he replied. "But I see your grandmother. That's a win."

Miss Bess giggled. "Doesn't Tommy say the nicest things?"

"Yes, he does. You're a very sweet man. Be good to my grandma now," she warned him with a grin. Grand Bess had giggled. It might be love. Again.

Before Tommy could answer, Miss Bess pulled him away. "Let's get that table over there. It's almost time for the concert. Come on, Honey."

At least she wouldn't be watching the concert alone.

As soon as they were seated, Miss Bess leaned in to whisper, "Ah saw you talkin' to Eli, What'd he say?"

Maybe alone would be better.

"We just chatted, Grand. He came to meet up with a friend, Rick Collins."

"He'll be back to you before this night is ova, Sugha."

Honey nodded, moved a finger over her lips as the music started. She could see Cricket standing front row center with a group of her friends cheering the group on and wildly flirting with the band members as only she could do.

After a minute, Honey recognized Rick Collins, even with his big shaggy beard. He played the bass guitar as he had in high school. She remembered that when he played ball with Eli they'd been the best of buddies. The Collins Brothers' music was similar to a popular country music band's sound. Caught up in the music, Honey toe tapped and hummed along. She relaxed for the first time in days, no, maybe weeks. The music chased away her worries. She was not worried about leaving town as soon as possible, not worried about losing the big story, not worried about being killed. The only suspects on her list attending the concert were Rachel and Ace. And they did have her attention.

Honey had spotted them minutes ago. The odd

couple seemed to be fighting nonstop. They were at a table just three away from Honey, Miss Bess, and Tommy. Rachel jabbed a finger toward Ace's chest. Ugly-frowning, he reared his body back so that he was in danger of falling backward on his chair. She watched them until they got up and disappeared into the standing crowd. She didn't attempt to follow the two. By then, the music had invaded her soul.

Although Honey lingered after the concert ended, she did not see Eli again. Most likely he and Rick had gone off together again. She decided to return to the *Banner Bay* offices and write up the exciting concert story. Determined to track down the black truck, the concert report would be one less thing for her to do the next day. She wrote the article, a brief one, and fell asleep at her desk. Something she used to do in Boston when she worked fifteen-hour days.

A siren woke her. Or was she dreaming? Blurry eyed, she blinked. No, a siren close by. She jumped out of her chair and ran to the door. She smelled smoke as soon as she opened the door. Even with only the light from the moon she could see smoke billowing from the Blue Oyster Grill. The town's two fire engines were parked outside. Cars with the volunteer brigade were pulling up. Grabbing her recorder, she ran to the grill, no easy task in her miniskirt.

Thea and Carol huddled together at the gas station across the street.

Eli and Leon stood among the fire fighters who had aimed their hoses at the kitchen.

"What's going on? What happened?" Breathless from her sprint, Honey puffed her questions to Eli.

"Fire in the kitchen. Probably grease. It's common

for restaurants."

"Carol smelled the smoke right off, called 911, and got Thea out. She moved so quickly we don't think there's much damage," Leo added. "Just a lot of stinky smoke."

"They were getting ready to open the restaurant again," Honey said.

"Might be a small delay," Eli remarked with a wry twist of his lips.

"Poor Thea. Can anything else happen to her?"

Eli turned his gaze from the fire to Honey. "Yeah. I feel for her too. I wouldn't go asking her any questions right now if I were you."

"I'm not totally insensitive," she snipped, stung. "When will you make an official report?"

"We'll go in with the fire department after the area cools down and see what we can find."

"An official investigation." Although she didn't say it aloud. Honey was thinking another insurance claim.

"Fire Marshal from Tallahassee has the last say. You might wait rather than speculate."

"I intend to, of course. And I'm going to attribute your snarkiness to having had a long stressful day with only a short concert respite."

"You think I'm snarky?"

"Yes."

"You must bring it out in me."

"When he's elected mayor, he won't be so uptight," Leon put in.

"Are you going to run for mayor? Have you decided then?" Honey asked.

Eli nodded. "Might. A few folks have been encouraging me to run."

"When are you going to announce?"

He shrugged. "Another story. Am I your only source of stories?"

"No, but I get why you'd think so." In the hopes that flattery would get her somewhere, she brazened ahead. "You're the most interesting person, man or woman in town."

"Like Leo says, the job might be a bit less stressful than this one."

"You'd make a great mayor."

"I have your vote then?"

"Yes. I'll even campaign for you."

"Hmmm." He nodded. "I like the sound of that."

"Me too. I'll order buttons and banners…"

"Don't get carried away. I haven't definitely decided yet."

She gave him a sheepish smile. Yes, sometimes she still bent to her impulsive streak. "Goodnight Eli…Leo."

****

Eli watched her go. Seems he'd watched Honey go many times, both literally and figuratively. She still possessed the same sweet figure and strong-willed personality that had captivated him originally. He hadn't found the strong-willed aspect as charming since they had been pitted against each other over the murders of Chef Andy and Don Turner. Who would have thought they'd come to this? Hometown sheriff and reporter. Oil and water. And yet…his stomach didn't squeeze shut when he saw her coming anymore. Instead, a warning warmth surged through him when her silver-blue gaze fixed on him.

He wondered if becoming mayor would put their relationship in a better place. He wondered if he even wanted that. She'd hurt him once. Badly.

Damn! Honey Mayhew stole into his thoughts like a bad dream when he had a million other things more important to think about.

Eli was torn. The town had the smallest budget on the Forgotten Coast. Most likely he'd be expected to serve as mayor and sheriff. Two jobs. Could he handle both as well as take care of his father and give Krystal more time? Eli liked his job as sheriff. He liked helping the folks of his hometown, liked solving mysteries—not that they came along too often.

Lately, Krystal had been demanding more of his time. She'd begun pushing for marriage. He wasn't sure but thought her new pressure might have something to do with Honey's return. He understood. Sometimes without warning, spotting Honey across a crowd in her wonky straw hat, that old feeling crept over him. The buzz of when they'd been young and in love. He chuckled softly; sparring with her, laughing with her tonight before the fire had been almost like old times. There it was again! She'd slid into his thoughts without warning.

"Somethin' funny?"

"No, Leo, nothing at all."

"We gonna take Thea to the Inn to spend the night?"

"Yeah. Let's go. We'll come back to the fire scene first thing in the morning."

****

Fred was waiting for Honey when she climbed the stairs, exhausted and happy to be home. The slight bounce to her step had more to do with Eli than the lights. Though she was reluctant to admit it, the chance she and Eli could at least be friends made her heart beat faster.

They'd taken a baby step towards reviving their friendship tonight.

She'd solved the frightening pitch-dark blackness problem last week. Flood lights had been installed all around the house and she always left lights on when she left in the morning. Still, she felt uneasy. Fred was not a watchdog. And this house was remote, hidden by high pines on one side…the bay on the other. Anyone could approach by the highway or the bay. Just about everyone who lived in town owned one type of boat or another.

Fred padded after her as she headed toward the bedroom. She froze in the doorway.

"Oh, no! No!"

Her mobile office set up in the corner of the room had been vandalized. Her personal laptop was on the floor. Hacked to pieces. Papers she'd printed were scattered everywhere. Some crumbled and she was fairly certain, many missing. Her research, her theories, everything she'd gathered on the Andy Mueller case lost, if not for the thumb drive in her pocket.

Her life and her family's lives had been threatened and her home vandalized, and her privacy invaded. Who was behind this? And what would be next? An icy shudder shook her body. "This is my home, Damn it! I will not be intimidated!" Honey did not merely scream aloud, she shrieked. "I will not be run out of my home!"

Chapter 13

Fire and Ice. Honey's belly burned with anger. No one had the right to invade her home and rummage through her personal property. She was a journalist doing her job. Fury quickly drove out any fear she might have felt. No one was going to scare her off. Even a killer. This was her home, her town. She vowed to stay in the Bay for the rest of her life, or until she found her nemesis. And wrote *The End* to the story.

Fred wagged his tail.

Jamming Eli's old red baseball cap on her head as if it were a warrior's helmet, Honey set to work. First, she attacked the mess and then began straightening and reorganizing her corner home office. Still buzzing with adrenalin, she emptied and stored two of the large boxes stacked in the dining area since her move back to the Bay. When she'd finished, only one box remained unpacked.

In the early hours of the morning, finally exhausted, she crawled to the bed and fell into a troubled sleep. She tossed and turned. Miss Bess floated through her nightmarish scenarios warning Honey about her drying eggs. Eli laughed when she confronted him, forcefully objecting to his marrying Krystal. Anyone else would do. Honestly, she'd asked him, had he considered marrying MaryLu? In the next disturbing scene, she attempted to call Eli to warn him not to marry Krystal. No answer, the phone kept ringing. Incessantly. She refused to give up.

But wait. Her groggy mind rose up through a thick cloud of sleep. Her cell phone *was* ringing. With one eye opened, she grappled on the bedside table until she found the cell.

"Good morning, Honey." The soft intimate greeting warmed her, a whisper of promise in her ear.

But no.

"Eli?" She bolted upright in the bed. Wide awake.

"Didn't wake you, did I?"

"No. No." Deny, deny. One denial overlapped the other. "What's up?" She glanced at the clock. Ten o'clock. She'd overslept thanks to her nightmare of a night.

"Thought you'd like to know we arrested Ace Barone for starting the fire at the Blue Oyster Grill."

"Um, yes, yes. Good to know. Thanks for the call." *Eli had actually called her with important news on the case.* "How did you catch him?"

"Carol Kahn came to the office this morning. She said Ace had been coming around the last few days asking for his old job back. Didn't take it too well when Thea and Carol said no. He threatened to shut the Grill down for good."

"Wow. An obvious motive. Did he resist arrest?"

"Nah. Found him in the River Bar too drunk to run. Apparently he'd been drinking all night since his chat with Thea and Carol."

"Has he confessed?"

"No. Don't expect him to, but we found all the evidence we need in his room. He had enough goods to burn the whole town down."

"Is he in the jail now?"

"Yeah. Not too happy either."

Honey couldn't believe Eli was actually answering all her questions. This was her opportunity to tell him about the threats against her and Cricket. Instead, she asked, "May I interview him?"

"You can, sure, but I don't know how cooperative he'll be. And just so you know, he's being transferred to Tally this afternoon."

"I'll be right there."

The line went dead. That was Eli. As far back as Honey could remember, he'd never said goodbye. He just hung up when the conversation ended. "Goodbye, Eli," she whispered.

Forty-five minutes later, she walked through the small combination sheriff's office and jail. On the way, she definitely decided to tell Eli about the threat against her, Cricket and the break-ins. Only Eli wasn't there.

"Had to go see his dad," Leo told her as she looked around. "Center called him."

She nodded. "I came to interview Ace."

Ace stood up and walked rather wobbly to the bars of the small cell as Honey approached. She took out her phone and pushed record. "Good morning, Ace."

"What do you want?" He smelled of garlic, stale beer, and cigarette smoke.

Honey backed up. She'd been standing too close to the cell. "I want to know if you started the fire at the Grill and if you did, I want to know why."

"Get lost."

"You've been caught. The sheriff has evidence you set the Grill on fire."

"Lady, he ain't proved nothin' yet." He turned away.

"You might as well talk. You've been caught."

Ace didn't bother to turn around. "Geez, are you still here?"

"I saw you arguing with Rachel last night. What was that about?"

"None of your business." Closing his eyes, he sat down heavily on the thin mattress of the cell's cot.

"You should know I'm working on the Chef Andy story as well. I will find out who killed him…and Donald Turner."

"Well, hell, don't look at me. I'm not your guy."

"Some folks think it might have been you that killed Andy. He fired you."

"Yeah, he did. I told you that."

"And so did Rachel just last night. She fired you."

"You're guessin,' lady."

Honey felt like she was on a roll. She was guessing but her guesswork was hitting home from the expression on Ace's face. His scowl said everything. Confident, she continued. "After Rachel fired you for who-knows-what, you went back to Thea. But she wouldn't give you your job back, so you tried to burn the Grill down."

He shook his head in a continuous motion. "Nope. You got it all wrong."

"Then set me straight. If you'd like to tell your side of the story and get it printed front page in *the Banner*, talk to me. You can let the whole town know you're innocent."

Cupping one side of his mouth, Ace shouted, "Leo, get this woman outta here."

"If you're innocent—"

"Lady, go away. I don't wanta talk to you and nothin' in the law says I have to be answerin' to you. You're a writer, right?"

So much more than that. "I am an investigative reporter and journalist."

"Get lost, lady. Get lost. Go write somethin'."

Shooting him her best if-looks-could-kill glare, Honey gave up on the town lowlife, turned on her heel and stalked off. No question in her mind that he started the fire. Eli had the evidence. But she couldn't see Ace as a murderer. Killing Chef Andy seemed a reach for a man who lacked backbone. And why would he go after Donald Turner?

She lowered her voice when she approached the deputy. "Leo, does Ace drive a black truck?"

He shrugged. "Don't think he owns anything."

"Do you know anyone around town who does drive a black truck?"

"Who doesn't is the question."

"What?"

"Everyone and his brother drives a macho black truck."

"Right." Shoving her phone into her backpack with a heavy sigh, Honey gave him a wave on her way out. "I'll see you later."

"'Kay. Say hello to Miss Bessie for me."

****

The last person Eli expected to see at the Senior Center's Nursing Care wing was Honey Mayhew. Like a fresh summer breeze, she hurried down the stark hall that smelled of death, decay, and disinfectant. He stood as she reached the hard wood bench where he'd been sitting. "Honey, what are you doing here?"

"How's your dad? Leo told me you'd been called about your dad. How is he?"

Shrugging, he released a weary breath. "I don't

177

know. No one has told me anything yet. I'm waiting for the doctor."

"Do you mind if I wait with you?"

"You're not going to talk about Barone, Andy, or Turner, are you?"

"No. I won't talk about anything…unless you'd like me to."

"No." He shook his head and gave her a rueful smile.

Silence descended on the hallway. The tile floor was cool and clean. Someone groaned from behind a nearby closed door. Machines from nearby rooms beeped and whooshed like an off-key electronic symphony.

Eli thought of the many times they had sat in silence together. Sometimes they'd just watched the tide roll in, sometimes watching pelicans dive for dinner. Sometimes, they were just thinking about where to go for a bite to eat following a game. But often it has just been the companionable silence of a strong connection. Like now?

"Have you emptied out any boxes lately?" he asked.

"Yes, as a matter of fact I emptied and stored the contents of two very large boxes last night."

"Have you done any painting? You mentioned you might paint the house."

"No. I'm…I'm still deciding on colors."

"When you decide, I'll help you. With the painting."

She angled her head regarding him with a puzzled expression. "Really?"

"Really."

"I'd like that." She smiled, a wide smile that reached her silver-blue eyes and added a dazzling sparkle. "I'll need help."

"You were never too handy, as I remember."

Still smiling, she nodded. "You remember correctly."

A door opened down the hall and a young nurse and older doctor approached them. Eli stood; Honey stood up beside him.

"Doctor Lyle. How's my dad?"

"Sit down, sit down," Lyle urged. The doctor, medium height and in his early sixties, possessed a distinguished look. Graying temples, deep crevices at the corners of his brown eyes, and rimless glasses marked him as a man to be respected.

"What's happened?" Eli asked.

"Sit down and let's talk for a minute."

The antiseptic, tense atmosphere sparked a nervousness foreign to Eli. He sat, feeling oddly comforted to have Honey sitting beside him.

"Eli, your dad has suffered a stroke. A mild one. But we need to talk about where to go from here." He glanced at Honey for a moment. "Perhaps this should be a private conversation."

"She can…Honey can listen."

Doctor Lyle nodded. "Since this is a mild stroke, we can treat him here. But he can get advanced care and benefit from it, in Tallahassee. An important difference is that you're here. You live here, work here, and can visit him frequently."

Eli rubbed his jaw. He felt the sharp stubble, felt the roiling anguish in his gut. "But he doesn't even know me half of the time."

"But the other half of the time he does. He knows he has a visitor, someone who cares for him. Someone who sees him every day, brings him candy and his favorite orange soda."

"But could he get better faster in Tallahassee? Is that what you think?"

"There are no guarantees. Your dad has been dealing with dementia for the last few years and now has had a stroke. Eli, you're his lifeline. No matter what you decide, know that there's no wrong or right decision. But you are the only one who can decide."

Eli lowered his head. His heart shrunk inside his chest. His foggy mind played the scenes of his dad playing ball with him as soon as Eli could hold a ball. He took a deep breath. "Stay. I…I think he should stay where I can see him regularly. He seems to like it when I take him walking by the bay. I think he'd miss the people and places that are familiar to him. On those somedays."

"All right then." The doctor stood. "We'll transfer Bill to the rehab care unit and start him on therapy this afternoon. Why don't you come by later around dinner time?"

"I can't see him now?"

"A visit now might be more stressful for him. We'll get him settled and start a routine."

"Thank you."

"See you 'round," he smiled. "Honey, say hello to your mom for me."

"I will."

A mixture of confused emotions rushed through Eli as he watched the doctor and his nurse walk back down the hall. Did he make the right decision for his dad? Or was he being selfish keeping him here, in town where he could see his dad every day?

"You did the right thing, Eli," Honey said softly, as

if she'd read his mind. "Your dad loves you. He needs to be near you."

"I hope. It's hard. Hard to know." Unable to hide the unshed tears blurring his vision, Eli stood; exposed and vulnerable. He'd never allowed anyone to see his inadequacy, his pain this deep, this close-up. But now.... God, he loved his dad. And he was powerless to help him.

Honey's hand, warm, and comforting, slipped into his. "Your dad's illness has to be difficult for you. If it were Momma or Miss Bess, I don't know what I would do. But I do know Bill needs you and this town more than what any medical center can offer."

"I don't want my dad to suffer, Honey, but I'm not ready to lose him altogether yet either."

"I understand. You won't lose him. He's always been a strong man. Do you remember when that storm blew up when we were in high school, and he was out tonging for oysters? The wind and water destroyed the dinghy but not your dad. He swam through those rough waters to shore."

"I'd almost forgotten that. Man, was I scared. But you were there, weren't you?"

"You swam out to help him. He made it in because of you."

"I was scared out of my mind."

"But you didn't let that stop you."

"You know, after Mom left us, he took to drinking, staggering home night after night so drunk he could barely stand upright. There were years when I hated him."

"You were disappointed in him."

Eli nodded. "And grateful when he stopped. When

181

he became my dad and friend again."

"You Gibson men have been through a lot together."

He nodded before gazing down at her. Her warm gaze met his. "Thanks, Honey. Thanks for coming. For waiting with me. You didn't have to."

"It's what friends do." She gave him a hurried hug.

Eli experienced a lost, floundering feeling. The brief hug when her body brushed against his ignited a desire to touch her. He stood like a robot. Rigid. Unwilling to do or say anything that might ruin the delicate balance they'd achieved.

Searching for something to say, the right thing, he cleared his gone-dry throat, but before he could speak, Honey did. "You'd better get back to the office, Sheriff. Ace Barone is a surly character that gave me no help at all."

"Don't say I didn't warn you."

"You did. And now you have to work your magic on him and get a confession."

"What are you going to do?"

"Go back to the office and see what my mother the editor has in the way of assignments for me."

"Give her my best, and Miss Bessie."

****

Honey left the community center, her heart heavy with sadness. One foot in front of the other. Her heart ached for Eli. After his mother left, Honey watched Eli suppress his sorrow by concentrating on trying to help his father and playing ball fourteen hours a day rain or shine. His world then revolved around his dad. She knew Bill was the reason he'd returned to the Bay. And she couldn't add to Eli's worries by telling him about her troubles. The threat, the break-in. She could and would take care of her own problems.

Today she had been there when he needed her. Chasing after her career even in college, she hadn't always been there for him. She'd read about his career-ending injury in the newspaper. Her mother had told her when Eli joined the Navy.

Her step grew lighter as she turned the corner and headed toward the newspaper office. Her mother, the editor waited for her.

"Honey, do you mind writing Miss Bess's senior column today?" Laura asked. She'd covered her hand over the mouthful of the sandwich she was eating at her desk.

"I just sat down."

"And I'm so glad you're here."

"Where is Grand?"

"She's having a long lunch with her new beau."

"Oh. Okay, but I have another, more important story. Ace Barone was arrested for setting the fire at the Grill."

"What? Why? Why would he do such a thing? He might have burned the Grill to the ground." Her mother never could seem to accept flat out evil in a person.

"Seems like he had an altercation with Carol and Thea. My theory is that he wanted his job as chef back and they tossed him out."

"Oh, my. What's this town coming to? Blue Oyster Bay used to be such a peaceful, charming little town."

"And now it's a hotbed of murder and mayhem."

"Sarcasm is unnecessary," she snipped before adopting a whole new tone. "Honey…"

Her mother's pause signaled a need for attention. "Yes?"

"You know you have the basics, the journalistic instincts to make a brilliant editor and publisher of *the Banner*."

Honey's nerves tingled a warning. "Um…I don't know about brilliant, Momma."

"I'm counting on you, along with your sister when the time comes."

The tiny hairs on the back of Honey's neck stood at attention. "Do you…are you serious about retiring or leaving *the Banner* to Cricket and me to run?"

Her mother smiled, her beautiful, sweet smile, almost beatific. "*The Banner* is your legacy."

"But—"

"And you won't have to wait until I die. I may retire…sometime soon. I've been thinking about taking some time for myself. I'm tired."

It didn't happen often, but Honey was at a loss for words. "Well, but, ah…you certainly deserve a, well, at the very least a vacation."

"When I retire you can do what you wish with the newspaper, go digital, buy new computers."

"Momma, I don't know as I'm—"

"I couldn't trust anyone but you with the family's baby. My only request is that you keep the newspaper in paper form for the folks who don't have digital access."

Honey nodded. Her head exploded. A churning deep in the pit of her stomach warned her if she accepted her inheritance, she would be trapped forever in the town she'd worked so hard to leave. She changed the subject. "How do you feel about Ace Barone's arrest as tomorrow's lead?"

"Of course."

But Honey started writing her stories with a nod to

the Senior Center, inviting readers to send cards to Bill Gibson who was recovering from a mild stroke. Which reminded her. "Momma, did I mention Bill Gibson suffered a stroke this morning?"

"No. Oh, my goodness. Poor Bill. Poor Eli."

"Eli decided to keep him at the Lighthouse, which Doctor Lyle didn't advise but strongly suggested."

"I'll go visit Bill as soon as I'm finished here."

Laura always did the right thing. "He'd appreciate seeing you."

"Send the fire story to me as soon as you can."

"No problem." Honey worked quickly for the next thirty minutes and finished just as the wail of sirens rent the air.

"A jail break!" Cricket cried, bursting through the door and running for the camera sitting on her desk.

"Here come your stories, Momma." Honey hit the send button, slapped on her straw hat, and followed Cricket running out the door.

By the time they reached the sheriff's office the culprit—Ace—had been captured.

Leo was locking the cell, mumbling. The prisoner made his way to the cot in his cell swearing beneath his breath, but loud enough for all to hear.

Cricket snapped a picture of Ace, lying on his back with his hands over his face. "False alarm, Leo?"

"Yeah. I brought his lunch tray, he whacked it out of my hands and ran for the door. I hit the alarm and gave chase. Caught up with him two blocks away. Good thing he was hungover and couldn't move very fast."

"Good thing," Honey repeated.

"Do you need more pictures?" Cricket asked.

"No."

"Then I'm done here," she said and left.

"Are you all right, Leo?" Honey asked. The deputy still gasped for air after his chase.

"Just embarrassed."

She was about to ask Eli's whereabouts when he stalked through the door. Krystal flitted in on his heels. Krystal. Krystal looked model elegant, as always, wearing a pink designer sundress, huge, movie-star sunglasses, and a wide-brimmed straw hat.

Dressed in a tee-shirt and cut-off jeans, Honey looked like a vagrant compared to Krystal. Suffering from a sudden crisis of confidence, she inched toward the door.

"What the hell happened, Leo?" Eli swore through tight lips.

"Sorry, boss. He slipped away when I brought his lunch tray, but I caught him soon enough."

"Is that your lunch on the floor too?"

"Yeah."

"After you clean up the mess, take an hour lunch break. "

"Thanks, Boss."

"I was in Rae Jean's diner when I heard the sirens. Got out as soon as I could."

"He was with me," Krystal added unnecessarily.

Swiping a hand across his sweaty forehead, Eli sat down and motioned for Krystal to take the lone seat across from his desk.

Forcing a smile, Honey backed up to the door. Just a quick turn and she would be out of the office.

"Honey?" Eli's tone stopped her in her tracks. "What are you doing here?"

"Answering the call of the sirens."

He chuckled.

"I'm happy you're here," Krystal said. "You'll be the first to know. Eli is going to run for Mayor of Blue Oyster Bay and I'm moving here to be his campaign manager."

No! Honey's mind screamed, but when she could find her voice, her mouth said, "Welcome to the Bay."

Chapter 14

Welcome to the Bay. Had she said that? Really said that?

Yes, she had. And then Honey had fled the sheriff's office faster than the Most Wanted monster on the FBI criminal list. She had not even been able to manage a glance at Eli on her way out. *He'd know. He'd recognize her tone. Polite but insincere.* With an ambiguous wave of her hand, she was out the door and racing toward her scooter.

Fury burned in the pit of her stomach, fury she had no right to feel. Honey slapped on her helmet, turned on the ignition and tore out of the parking lot in a spray of sand and broken oyster shells.

She should be Eli's campaign manager. She knew the sheriff better than Krystal. She'd known him since they were kids. And she knew the people, knew the town, what it needed and what Eli could offer.

Turning on to Main Street, she slowed. Why was she so angry? OMG, could it be she was jealous of Krystal, the outsider's supermodel figure and designer wardrobe? Or was she emotionally disturbed because it appeared that Eli was in love with Krystal? Why else would he give her the trusted position of campaign manager? But worse, none of what Eli was doing with his personal life should matter. She was over him. He was over her.

If Honey allowed herself to get all emotional, she

couldn't concentrate on the story. And since talking with Cricket, the most important thing was to find the scraped black pickup truck before anyone else was seriously hurt. Or dead.

She drove to Rachel's restaurant and into the parking lot. Fortunately, it wasn't necessary to confront Rachel. One of the oyster shuckers, taking a smoke out back, pointed to his employer's ride, a convertible. The one black truck in the parking lot was in pristine condition and sported a vanity plate, Gil & Maria. The shine almost blinded her.

Next, Honey drove to Ace's motel. The teen registration attendant laughed. "Man, he walks. He don't have a nickel to his name. How could he afford a ride?"

"Silly question. Sorry to have woken you up."

She didn't find a black pickup truck behind the Blue Oyster Grill either, so she took another tact and motored to Hal's Auto Repair, Collision and Drive-thru Wash. Hal owned the only auto repair business in town. No one was around so Honey hopped off her scooter and moseyed around the three bays, hoping not to attract attention. Sure enough, she found what she was looking for in the third bay. The black pickup with a six-foot, nasty looking scrape down the passenger side. Cricket had done herself proud. Even if it has been a crazy thing to do. Honey hurried into the office. Air conditioned by a window mounted unit which barely cooled the place down, the small space with the cement floor smelled of grease and sardine sandwiches.

"Hal?"

A burly guy, Hal had the grizzly look obtained with a three-day shadow of a beard and enhanced with black greased hands. Narrowing his gaze on her, he put down his sandwich and swung his feet off the desk. He didn't appear to be the brightest bulb in town. "Yeah?"

"I see you're working on a black pickup truck. What's wrong with it?"

"What's it to ya?"

"A truck like that almost ran my sister off the road the other day."

"Sorry to hear that."

"So what are you doing to it?"

"A little repair work."

"Obviously. Whose truck is it?"

"Turner's."

Honey started. "Turners? Donald Turner?"

"Yeah. You remember him? Running for mayor. Drowned not too long ago."

"How did you get his truck?"

"He left it to a friend who wants to sell it."

"Who's the friend?"

"Can't tell you that. Confidential."

She nodded, then quickly asked, "When will it be ready for Carol to pick up?"

"Tomorrow."

Honey smiled. Okay, maybe it was a smirk. This little trick had worked for her before. Hal responded automatically before he'd had a chance to think about it. "Thanks, Hal."

The auto repair guy had just named Carol as the driver of the black pickup. The vicious woman had attempted to drive Cricket off the road. Honey's little sister! On the one hand, Honey's belly bubbled with acidy anger, and on the other, a swell of pride swooshed through her veins for handily solving the mystery of the black pickup.

The time had come to connect the dots. First, back to the newspaper and then she'd be off to the sheriff's office to share what she discovered with Eli. She'd certainly win points with him for this information, the information that would give him the killer. Honey planned to be at his side to watch him make the arrest. Thinking of Eli's reaction, led her to other thoughts of the Bay's splendid sheriff.

If Eli had ever loved Honey, how could he now be in love with someone so different than her? What attracted one person to another? Was it undefinable chemistry? Appearance? Was it common interests? Or was it just simply a case of opposites attract?

Honey's relationship with Mark, the journalist who dumped her several months ago, was based on mutual interests. They both pursued journalist careers to the exclusion of life. Mark's ambition matched hers and was very different from Eli. Eli loved her when he played baseball and all she'd known about the game was the 7th inning stretch. He pitched for the high school team, she wrote the sports column and the school news for the Blue Oyster Bay High School Bulletin. When she'd tried out for the girls' high school softball team thinking to please Eli, she'd been rejected. He comforted her, emphasizing her writing talent. In truth, and to this day, Honey possessed the athletic ability of a sloth.

The men in her life were different in appearance as well. Mark was handsome in a cute boy next door sort of way. Eli always had been more rugged in build and features. While Mark possessed a stinging sense of humor, her first love possessed deep-rooted kindness that sometimes, in retrospect, she had mistaken for weakness. Eli gave people the benefit of the doubt, unlike Mark, a judgmental man who often dissed folks based on nothing more than gut feelings. The reporter was unapologetically ruthlessly ambitious and, foolishly, she'd admired his endless work ethic. Still, Honey had been working on gentling him some. Until he dumped her. The truth of who was the better man was as clear to her now as was high tide. And way too late.

She pulled up behind the *Banner* office, stopping with a jolt.

"Lordy, you came in hot." Miss Bess opened the back door. "Somethin' botherin' you?"

"No, no, Grand, I just got a bit distracted."

"Can Ah help?"

"No, but thanks. Are you leaving?"

"Sugha, ah have a date with Tommy. He's takin' me out to dinner and then the theater."

"Wow. You move fast, Grand."

"Don't have time to move slow at my age. Ah'll give you a full report tomorrow."

"Can't wait."

"Ah think he's the one," she whispered, and winked.

"Oh, my," Honey muttered, turning away just in time to bump into her mother. "Momma, are you leaving too?" It was unheard of for Laura to leave the newspaper early.

"Yes, I'm going to swing by and see Bill Gibson on the way home."

"Thanks, Momma."

"What are you doing tonight? Would you like to come to dinner?"

"No, thanks. I…I have plans."

"Okay, then. Goodnight. Love you."

"Love you too. Bye."

Alone in the office, Honey reviewed her plans. She slammed her backpack down and sank into her computer chair. She was pretty certain she knew who had killed Chef Andy and Donald. The sooner the killer was in jail the better.

Solving the murders, writing, and selling the story were more important than ever. She had to get out of town quickly before she was trapped, before life became more complicated. Such as when her mother announced her retirement as editor of the Banner Bay. And Krystal announced her engagement to Eli.

Honey realized she was incapable of watching from the sidelines as Eli ran for mayor and especially when he was sworn in, which he certainly would be. He had been the town hero for years.

And lastly, she refused absolutely and unequivocally to be in town when wedding bells rang for Eli and Krystal. Her decision wasn't based on envy or loss or heartbreak. She was being practical. Her heavy heart had nothing to do with her refreshed resolve.

The best way possible for her to accomplish her goal was to dig deep and revive her old and tired ambition. Her ticket out of the Bay was to have a major story published nationwide.

After spending another hour in the office reviewing her previous stories and notes on Chef Andy and Donald Turner's deaths, Honey decided to follow her gut. Dusk had descended when she pulled her faithful scooter up behind the Blue Oyster Grill. Before she banged on the back door, she removed her helmet and set her phone to record.

Thea opened the door. "Honey?"

"Can we talk, Thea?"

"No, we're cleaning up the fire mess. We have a contractor coming tomorrow morning."

"This won't take long." Honey intended to cut to the chase quickly. No more Miss Nice-and-Polite-*Bay Banner* reporter.

"No. No, I said. I don't have time." Thea's dark eyes narrowed, her tone deepened to more of a mutinous growl than her normal sweet voice. "The Grill reopening has already been delayed by the freakin' fire. So, just get out of here, Honey, and leave me alone."

"One last question."

Thea rolled her eyes but did not shut the door.

"Do you know who killed your husband?"

"What?"

Obviously stunned, Thea's frown creased every little line from her forehead to the brackets around her mouth, which dropped open.

Honey stared her down. She knew most people think it's a crazy question to directly ask a person of interest if they killed the victim. But it's a technique used frequently by law enforcement and enterprising journalists. Often, caught off guard by the blunt question, the suspect answers without thinking. And answers truthfully.

"You do, don't you?" Honey pressed, taking a step closer.

"You're trespassing," Thea shrieked. Her cheeks flushed with anger. "Get off my property now! I'm filing a restraining order against you, you...you bitch."

Before Honey could reply to the unexpected rant, Carol came up behind Thea. Honey smelled her first, the sweet, heavy perfume brought up a new round of nausea. Carol's steely granite eyes spit fire. If looks could kill,

Honey would be dead. "You again? You're tougher to get rid of than a hill of ants. Leave, Mayhew, before I call the cops." The heavy-set woman pushed Thea aside, then heaved her weight against the door, slamming it shut.

The little scene had resolved any doubts Honey may have had. It was time to share with Eli. She might only have circumstantial evidence, but she felt confident the sheriff's skills could close the case. When she pulled up to the police department's headquarters, she could only see Leo behind the desk. Elli wasn't there and neither was his car in the lot. She could wait. She felt reasonably confident that no one was going anywhere between now and tomorrow morning.

At home Fred greeted Honey with a lazy wag of his tail, but it was better than the receptions she'd received most of the day. She patted his head, whispered sweet nothings to him and poured a bowl of dog food. She made herself a bowl of cereal. Her favorite, protein flakes with yogurt.

Her gut had been speaking to her all the way home. Carol was the killer. Carol and Thea obviously hated her, and frankly she didn't care for either of them. Her sympathy for Thea had vanished. Singly the women gave her cold chills, together they posed a death threat.

She watched the news while having her dinner of cold honey oats cereal. But her mind wandered seeking a way to entrap Carol into a confession without getting herself killed. So far Honey's evidence was all circumstantial and Eli, not to mention a jury, might not accept it.

In Honey's mind, with the deaths of Chef Andy and Donald Turner, Carol had become the true operator of the Blue Oyster Grill. She'd manipulated Thea into a subservient position and stood to profit from the tourist popular restaurant as soon as it reopened. Quite a leap for a restaurant hostess, from server to owner.

"Come on, Fred. Let's take a walk on the beach." Honey stuck her phone in her back pocket." I'll think of something. I've got to think of something. I will think of something. And don't worry, when I leave Blue Oyster Bay, I'm taking you with me."

She strolled along the beach thinking, picking up shells, watching the stingrays gliding close to shore feeding. Sand tickled between her toes, the sea breeze swept through her hair. Sadness that weighed on her lifted, shifted to acceptance.

"Come on Fred, let's go back."

Her leisurely walk back to the house on the wet hard packed sand ended when they reached the path to the beach house. The lights in the main house lit up the night. Since the break-ins, Honey had put in timers. As dusk descended the lights whoosh on. She would never enter a dark house again, the only problem tonight being the cement pad level where the storage unit, parking, and stairs to the main house began was dark. The floodlights were out. "Aargh, something else to take care of, Fred." But her worry covered more than floodlights. A Killer was loose, and she had to run through the dark to reach the stairs to the house.

A tremble of fear shot through her, ending in a somersaulting stomach.

Fred barked as soon as they reached the pad.

"What's the matter, boy?"

He kept on barking.

Honey stopped in her tracks. She searched the dark

area looking for she knew not what.

And then she smelled it. And sneezed. Carol's perfume.

Shadows stepped out from beneath the stairs. Two shadows. Honey's first instinct was to turn and run but feared she wouldn't get far. She could scream for help, but no one would hear her. The next beach house was too far away to hear or see anything that happened here.

Honey's heart hammered against her chest. Her skin grew cold. "Hello? Who's there? I…I wasn't expecting company."

Carol stepped out of the shadows. She stood close enough for Honey to see she held a baseball bat by her side. The same bat that had clobbered poor Donald Turner unconscious?

Honey swallowed hard. She was about to die.

Chapter 15

Faking bravery she did not feel, Honey lifted her chin and confronted the overly-perfumed Grill hostess, and demanded in a wobbly voice, "What are you doing here?"

Carol smiled. "Now what do you think?"

"Who's with you?"

Before she could answer, Fred nipped one of Carol's fat ankles.

She sneered and kicked him.

"Just a minute," Honey snapped, galvanized by a surge of anger. "Leave my dog alone."

Whimpering, Fred lumbered to her side.

"Or what?" Thea asked, moving out of the shadows. She stood shoulder to shoulder beside Carol, blocking the stairway.

"Thea?" Not Thea. Honey shook her head, attempting to shake off disappointment and worse, fear. Her heart drummed. A yacht-sized knot lodged in her throat.

"Yes, it's me. I had you fooled, didn't I?" she asked with pride and a satisfied smile.

Honey decided to play dumb. "Fooled? I don't understand. What are you'all doing here? I left the Grill like you asked, when you asked."

"Getting tired of asking you to get out of our lives," Carol said. "And just so you know, we went to the

198

sheriff's office and took out a restraining order. No judge needed in emergency situations in our town."

"Oh? I didn't know. I'll honor the order. I…I promise." She forced a smile looking from one woman to the other. "You don't have to worry about me."

"We won't. Worry," Carol drawled.

"Ahh…ah…choo!" Honey found this encounter painful on so many levels. "What do you …you mean?" Another bigger, louder sneeze followed her question. Carol's perfume would kill her before the baseball bat was even swung.

"What's wrong with you?" Thea bit out. "You sound like an elephant."

"I'm, I'm allergic to …" she paused to shoot a death stare at Carol, "…your friend."

"Bitch."

Honey shook her head again. "Language, Carol."

"I'm through talking."

"Good." Honey's hutzpah was running low. She couldn't keep up the bravado much longer. Or the sneezing. It brought tears to her eyes and blurred her vision. Neither could she get the phone out of her pocket without alerting the women. All she could think to do was keep them talking. While she figured out how to get away from them. "Okay, you win. I won't come to the Grill anymore."

Was this any way to treat a customer?

Carol's half smile held no mirth. "You bet you won't."

"I won't even eat there when you reopen. Consider me warned and go home. Please."

The Grill's hostess shook her head. "Can't do that. You've already been warned several times."

"Thea, talk some sense into your friend. You can't get away with this."

"With what?" Thea asked in an all-innocent tone. "We can't be blamed if you take a tumble down the stairs in the dark." She sighed and *tsked*. "The accidents around the Bay are adding up."

"No one's going to miss you, your stupid red scooter and dumb straw hat," Carol added.

A bit spitefully, in Honey's opinion.

Honey gave a heavy sigh. She had nothing to lose. "Who killed Andy? Was it you, Carol?"

"No. It was me." Thea said, loudly and proudly.

"What?" Honey almost folded over from the wave of shock that hit her in the belly like a blow from a prizefighter.

"I had to kill him. He abused me until I couldn't take it anymore. Just sprinkled a little bit of arsenic here and a little there, slowly over the course of time. So it wouldn't come up in an autopsy." She shrugged her shoulders. "I had to do it, you see. In self-defense."

Honey seized on Thea's explanation. "You...you won't be prosecuted for self-defense. Turn yourself in."

Carol chuckled. "You must think we're a couple of Bay rednecks."

"Oh, no I don't," Honey assured her. "No, no."

"But you're wrong," Thea said. "And we won't let a spoiled bimbo like you ruin our plans."

Terrified, Honey's entire body shook. "Not spoiled. Not a bimbo."

"*Banner Bay* women thinking they're smarter and far above the rest of us," Carol clarified her thoughts in a sing-song voice.

"Oh, no," Honey quickly denied her accusation.

"Ah…ahchoo!"

"She's getting on my nerves," Thea told Carol.

Honey's time was running out. Her heart raced faster. Her pulse galloped. And the journalist who drove her ambition unexpectedly lurched into the fray. Fear forgotten. She needed answers before she died. "What about Donald Turner? Your partner? What happened to him? Did you…"

"That was me," Carol's boast came with an evil grin. "After I took care of the greedy SOB, he drowned. Thea and I were not interested in profit sharing."

"Got it." Honey swallowed. She got it in more ways than one. Neither of these women had any problem taking a life. They were killers. Her life flashed before her. She understood her last breath would be taken in pursuit of the story that would take her out of Blue Oyster Bay. And that was sad. Well, yes, she'd be leaving town, but not the way she planned. One of the women would hold her while the other swung the bat.

"And now that we've had this little chat, we're going to have to kill your nosy ass." Carol started to raise the bat.

Thea stepped forward. "But you finally got your story, right?" Thea added with a wry smile as she grabbed for Honey's hand. And missed.

Seemingly, all in one swift, fluid motion, Honey pivoted away and sprinted toward the water. Drowning or being shark bait seemed better than standing waiting to be killed. She only hoped she could outrun the women. She wasn't in great shape. Sorry now for all those vows she'd made to exercise more and then ignored.

Fred took to growling, waddling after the women as fast as possible for him. Honey looked over her shoulder to see Fred going for Carol's ankles again. But it was Thea of all people gaining on Honey. The widow's arms were pumping, her feet flying.

Panting and pushed to her limits, a silent mantra spun in Honey's head. *"Please, don't have a gun. Please, don't have a gun."*

To Honey's relief no shots rang out in the night. Apparently neither woman packed a weapon—other than the bat.

The night sky had closed in. The ocean and the night sky blended into one black canvas. A pale crescent moon was on the rise, hidden now and again by fast moving clouds. Honey quickly weighed her options. There were none.

She kicked off her flip-flops and hit the water running. She'd rather take her chances with the Gulf than Carol or Thea—the mad, bad murderous team of Blue Oyster Bay.

In an attempt to camouflage her movements Honey churned the warm bath water, spraying as much as she could around and behind her. Finally, she reached a depth where she could dive under the water and disappear. She'd opened her eyes underwater more times than she could count but not at night. The Gulf was a dark and dangerous world only fools dared enter after dusk. Better to close her eyes and swim. Keep moving.

She heard the women arguing. Shrill voices in the quiet of the night. Carol urged Thea to go into the water after Honey. Thea refused.

Relieved a bit, Honey swam parallel to the shore and south, away from the beach house and the hellcat killers. She held her breath as long as possible. One minute, two minutes. Her lungs were ready to burst before she had no choice but to poke her head out of the water and breathe. Breathing so hard her ribs hurt, Honey scanned the beach until she found the women. They were outlines standing close to the shore, watching, and waiting. Quiet now.

Were they waiting for her to drown? Were they watching for sharks to attack her?

The lunatic women were obviously determined to kill Honey one way or another. They would wait her out. Until dawn if necessary. Honey could not last that long.

Afraid to hold her head above the water for too long in case they spotted her, she'd backed herself into a watery corner, not knowing what the women could or would do. She struggled with anger and fear, with tears. Her stomach rolled over in knots. Her heart thundered in her chest. In an effort to calm herself, she took deep breaths, in through her nose, released through her mouth. As soon her breathing returned to normal, Honey filled her lungs once more and dove beneath the water again. She was growing tired.

Her arms had become cement blocks. She could barely lift them. She kicked beneath the water like a drunken sailor. When she surfaced again, she was farther out from shore and confident that the crazies could not see her. She could hardly see them. She feared she wouldn't have the strength to swim back to land. Treading water, tears streaming down her face, Honey hoped for a miracle.

And then it happened. A movement that distracted her would-be killers. Carol and Thea looked back at the beach house. Honey saw it then too. A red light flashed in the parking area beneath her beach house. Relief cursed through her. She heard the whoop-wail of a siren—and knew.

The sheriff had come to her rescue. She watched and wondered. How had he known? What was he thinking?

Eli knew he'd caught his suspects red-handed about to kill again. Honey. His Honey! The women took off, running down the beach toward a copse of pines where apparently they thought they could hide. But he and Leo were in better physical shape, and they ran much faster. Leo tackled Carol, sending her face down in a massive spray of sand. Eli simply seized Thea by the arm. They quickly cuffed the women and marched them back down the beach to the patrol car.

Honey slipped under the water once, twice, three times as she watched. She was so tired. Eli looked over his shoulder out to sea. Could he see her? He took something from the trunk of the car and ran back to the beach. "Honey! Honey! Are you out there?"

He turned on a floodlight and skimmed the water. He was operating the world's largest flashlight, searching for her, guessing she'd taken to the water. "Honey! Answer me!" His tone was panicked and urgent.

Pain shot through Honey's arms and legs as she maneuvered forward, toward the scene of the capture. Each shaky breath she took brought needles and pins and more pain. She wanted to *whoot whoot* the capture, but she was too weak to do even that. She raised one arm, an arm that weighed more than she did. "Here! I'm here, Eli!" Her call was weak.

But he heard her. The light reached her, blinded her before he threw it down, kicked off his shoes, unfastened his gun belt and ran into the water.

"I'm here! Eli, I'm here!"

He reached her quickly, taking her in his arms.

Warm, rescuing arms. He held her tightly against his body. Safe. Sheltered. Honey relaxed against him. Her weary heart beat a familiar tune, and it was not fear. She shivered from exhaustion as Eli carried her out of the bay. "My hero, my hero," she mumbled before passing out.

The next thing Honey knew, she woke in a warm bed, a hospital bed.

"How are you feeling?" Marylu stood by the bed.

"Tired. But alive."

She took Honey's hand. "You're very brave."

"Foolish maybe."

"Eli will be back soon. Can I bring you water…"

"No…I think I swallowed enough water tonight."

"Sorry."

"I'll just rest a minute before I go home."

But when she opened her eyes, Eli was sitting by her bed.

"Are you okay?"

"Just tired. I'm ready to go home now."

"I don't know if you should be alone."

"Thea and Carol? They're behind bars, aren't they?"

"No one will have to worry about them again."

"What made you come to the house?"

"They did. Thea came to the office to file a restraining order against you. First, I cannot issue those and second, I thought one of my persons of interest was protesting too much about the nosy reporter. I, ah, did an exciting stakeout."

"Thea was a suspect all along?"

"You know what they say, it's usually the spouse. In this case I didn't think she was up to planning and pulling it together by herself. So, yeah, I had my eye on Carol too."

"I should have known." Honey shot him a grin. How had she ever lost faith in Eli? This smart, strong, kind man was every woman's dream come true. She'd really messed up. Sighing, she threw the bedsheets back. "It's time for me to go home now."

"I'll drive you. You're not scooter-ready yet."

"Will you put on the siren?"

"No, but I will be sleeping on your couch. You have a couch, don't you?"

"Of course."

"And it's unpacked."

"Of course. I only have one box left to unpack."

Eli let out a long low whistle.

Honey nodded off on the ride home and again as soon as she rolled into bed fully clothed. She curled up safe and comfortable with Eli sleeping in the next room. Her ambition almost got her killed. Was any story worth her life? And yes, she did have a life in Oyster Bay. She had family and lifelong friends. How would her recklessness, or death have affected her mother, Cricket, and Miss Bessie? She would not, could not for the world hurt her family. There were other stories to write, other headlines to fly on *the Banner*.

She woke to the smell of freshly brewed coffee. After pouring herself a mug, she padded out to the porch where she found Eli. Fred lay at his feet.

"Great view you have here," he said.

"It is. I like it. I believe I'm going to stay and enjoy it every day."

"Really?"

"Yes. Really. I'm going to be the editor and publisher of *the Banner* someday."

He grinned. Happiness shone in the deep-blue indigo sea of his eyes. "I like the sound of that."

"Me too."

"You wouldn't publish gossip, would you?"

"Depends on the gossip. Do you have some for me?"

"Krystal has decided against moving to the Bay. She's not going to be my campaign manager if I run for mayor."

Honey ignored the sudden leap of her heart. At least she tried to. "I know I shouldn't ask, and your answer will be strictly off-record, but what happened?"

"We both realized that she wasn't cut out for small-town life. And like you, I'm not going anywhere. Krystal and I decided to remain friends and go our separate ways. She was taking this political thing way too seriously. She was thinking I should run for governor eventually."

Honey hoped Eli wasn't hurting over the breakup. He'd said he wanted to start a family pretty soon. And now the baby mama was gone. "I'm sorry, Eli. Are you feeling okay?"

"Yeah. Krystal was hanging onto the sports celebrity I used to be. Not certain she ever cared for me, small town sheriff."

I had the same feeling. But instead of saying what she thought, Honey simply said, "I'm sorry."

"It's for the best." He took a deep breath, turned to Honey. A soft smile played on his lips. "But there is one thing. I've come to an important decision and there's something I want to ask you."

The bottom of Honey's stomach dropped out. Her heart skipped several alarming beats. "Sure," she said as nonchalantly as possible. "What is it? Ask me anything."

"I've decided. I am going to be a candidate for mayor. Will you be my campaign manager?"

A word about the author…

Sandra Madden is a former writer/producer for a Miami PBS television station where she specialized in women's issues and public affairs programming. Before turning to writing full time, Sandra also held positions as a radio copy and promotion writer in both Miami and Los Angeles.

Ms. Madden is the published author of fifteen historical and contemporary romance novels, translated and issued in over 6 languages. She also co-authored "Reuben Kincaid Remembered," the memoir of her late husband Dave Madden, comedian and television actor, most well-known for his role as Reuben Kincaid on "The Partridge Family."

Currently, Sandra is a member of NINC, South Florida Fiction Writers and the Florida Writers Association.

www.sandramadden.com

Thank you for purchasing
this publication of The Wild Rose Press, Inc.

For questions or more information
contact us at
info@thewildrosepress.com.

The Wild Rose Press, Inc.
www.thewildrosepress.com